Thank you very much for purchasing this book.

Title Wild Hearts
Subtitle: Werewolf Romance Novel
Author: Rose Charles

Table of Contents

Wild Hearts
Description

Jessie Lewis is a 30 year old lady who's excited to begin her new job as a housekeeper for a billionaire recluse, Seth Irving. However, she has been told numerous stories of how Seth had chased away so many housekeepers. She will be the fifth one in a month. Jessie's mother resides in the hospital and is trying to treat her lung disease. With hospital bills piling up as a result of her mother's sickness, Jessie is trying her best to maintain her job.

Seth's cold demeanor puts Jessie off and she finds herself disliking the good looking but difficult, strange man. Slowly, Jessie gets involved in the complicated life of her boss and starts to notice some strange occurrences in the house. Seth asks Jessie to accompany him to an event and she realizes that she has fallen for the man she couldn't stand.

Things get strange at the event and Jessie realizes her life is in danger when she gets attacked by a pack of werewolves. Ambushed and hurt, Jessie fears that her life may have come to an end. Seth bursts into the middle of the rival wolf pack and before she passes out, she accidentally sees Seth change into his werewolf form. She detaches herself from him out of fear and swears to never go near him again. Unable to stay away, Jessie finds herself in Seth's life again. However, as Jessie gets tangled in Seth's dangerous world, she realizes why Seth is such a lone wolf. Could the cold man be lovable after all?

Chapter 1

"Mrs. Murray, here is your lemon drizzle cake and a Macchiato, warm, just the way you like it." Jessie Lewis smiled back at the elderly woman who beamed as she bit into her delicious cake.

Mrs. Murray had been coming to Jerry's Coffee Point years before Jessie started working at the small cake and coffee shop. Jessie served the sweet old woman her lemon cake and Macchiato every day for the five years she had been working there. Even though Jessie had told her to stop giving her tips, Mrs. Murray blatantly refused and handed her coins ritually.

"Jessie darling, how's your mother now?" Mrs. Murray looked up at her in concern.

Jessie looked around the coffee shop and saw that the few patrons were attended to. She glanced at the door leading to the storage, and it didn't seem like her boss was coming out soon, so she sat in the chair opposite Mrs. Murray. The scent of her Chanel No. 5 Eau Premiere enveloped Jessie, and she couldn't help but miss her mother.

"She's still in the same condition as before. The doctors said I need to pay the accumulating medical bills before they can perform another surgery on her."

Jessie felt tears rush to her eyes, threatening to flow down her smooth and pale face. To say she was stressed was to put it lightly. Jessie had begun taking double shifts and would have added a third one if Jerry's had allowed it.

Mrs. Murray put a jeweled and warm hand on Jessie's and gave her a soft smile. "Darling, you know I would love to help you. I can take out a loan and-"

Jessie leaned back, alarmed. "Gosh, no! Thank you so much, but I'll never allow you to do that. I'm sure I will find a solution soon."

Mrs. Murray shrugged, her white hair bobbing with the movement. "Alright, love. But remember, I'll love to help you."

Jessie smiled at her as she stood up. She nodded in appreciation and moved away just in time for her boss, Jerry, to walk out of the storage room. His face was clouded with worry and frustration. I glanced at Hailey, the only other waitress, as she was taking an order. She shrugged, clueless about what has happened.

Jerry ran his hand through his salt and pepper hair and abruptly punched the wall. Everyone was taken aback and stared at him incredulously.

"I'm sorry about that. Jessie, Hailey, please, I need to talk to you both."

Hailey glanced at Jessie with worry and mouthed, 'what is going on?'

Jessie shrugged because she genuinely didn't know what was going on. Her wavy bob was getting into her face, so she tried to twist her hair into a messy bun by removed the hair tie from her wrist.

They both walked into the store, and Jessie played with her apron nervously. Jerry was on a phone call, and he kept whispering ferociously to the other person on the line.

Hailey leaned towards Jessie and whispered, "Are we in trouble or something?"

"I have no idea. He seems nastier today. I didn't think that was possible."

Hailey giggled loudly, and jerry shot her a look till she quieted down. Jerry put his phone in his pocket and turned to face them.

Jerry was a big man, and his loud countenance went hand in hand with his large frame. However, for the first time, he looked weak and exhausted. His skin was ashy, and sweat gathered at his brows despite it being a fabulous evening. He balled his fists and stared at the ground.

Jessie's concern grew into worry, and she took a step towards him. "Is everything okay? What's going on?"

Finally, Jerry spoke. "We're shutting down."

The silence that followed felt like it was going to devour Jessie whole. She opened her mouth to speak, but no words seemed to form.

Hailey's voice cracked as she broke the silence, "But why? W-what's going on?"

Jerry rubbed his face, "I've been trying to save the shop, but there's nothing I can do. We're bankrupt."

Jessie swallowed the huge lump in her throat and spoke, "So what now?"

Jerry crouched to arrange some boxes that had toppled off the shelf. "I have sent Grace home. She won't be baking anymore. I should have told you both before now, but I was hoping some miracle will happen. I'm sorry, girls. I'll give you your pay for today. The shop has to be closed permanently by the end of the day."

Jessie absentmindedly touched her uniform. She had gotten familiar with the feel of cheap cotton on her skin ever since she turned twenty-five. The familiar faces of Mrs. Murray, the student who came mainly for the free Wi-Fi and other customers who had made Jerry's Coffee Point their go-to place for the delicious desserts that Grace always dished out daily.

Jessie felt another wave of panic when she realized that there was no way she could pay her mother's medical bills anymore.

She asked Jerry, "But is there anything we can do? We can ask for donations or-"

Jerry was already shaking his head as he interrupted her. "I'll never do that to my loyal customers. I can't collect their hard-earned money for this. I might as well take a break. It'll be good for me."

Hailey was barely holding back tears as she silently listened. Jessie rubbed the 23-year-old's back as she sniffled into a handkerchief. Hailey had been saving to afford her college, and Jessie felt overwhelming sympathy for the sweet girl.

For the first time, Jessie could see the reason behind Jerry's strictness and seemingly harsh attitude. Jerry had been running the coffee shop for twenty years since his divorce, and it was something he had put in so much work to build. He expected the best from everyone, which is why he was firm in his approach.

Jessie could say she was grateful to him for teaching her how to work under pressure, and she earned money to pay for her rent.

The day wasn't over, so Jessie went back to taking orders from customers who were glad to eat after a long day. Mrs. Murray had left when Jessie came out of the room, so she didn't get to say goodbye.

I wonder what she will think when we don't open tomorrow, Jessie thought. She was going to miss the sweet old woman for sure.

Jessie wasn't sure how Jerry would let everyone know the shop was shutting down, but she assumed he would be putting up a sign or something like that. She was going to miss the place. The way the floral wallpaper seemed to shine when it was sunset and the smell of coffee beans and cake mixing in the air. And now, all of it was gone.

Soon, the shop was emptying, and Jessie looked out the window; darkness had fallen faster than she had expected. Jessie pulled off her apron and finally felt the stress of the day. The double shifts were taking a toll on her.

She felt a touch on her shoulder and turned to look. It was Hailey.

"I'm going to really miss you. We should hang out sometime." Jessie leaned into Hailey's hug and realized how much she was going to miss her.

Hailey had brought her sparkle to the coffee shop, and Jessie found it endearing. Her dream of getting into UCLA and bagging a degree in economics, the way she would take out all the raisins in the muffins that Grace gave to them on their breaks, the crazy stories she always had about the various flings she got into. Jessie was really going to miss her.

"That's it, girls. Thank you for everything. Here's your pay for today." Jerry handed them their money and opened his mouth to speak. He changed his mind and gave them a brief smile.

"Bye, Jerry," Jessie said as she sadly returned the smile. Hailey waved at him, and they both drop their name tags before walking out of the shop.

"Take care." Jessie waved at Hailey one last time before walking away from the shop. She pulled out her cellphone and checked the time. It was 10:26 pm. It wasn't that late, but the streets were already quiet. The day had been warm, so Jessie didn't think to take a sweater or jacket.

She rubbed her arms as the chilly air sipped into her clothes. Albany's streets were littered with few people, but that was enough to put Jessie at ease. She didn't know why, but she felt nervous as the clanks of her boots echoed back to her.

Finally, she could see her apartment a little farther away. She hoped there was something she could, at least, microwave. She didn't have any energy to cook. A loud clanking interrupted Jessie's thoughts, and her head turned around quickly to see a bloodied dog baring its teeth at her.

Jessie froze and stared into the unusually bright blue eyes of the dog. It looked unusual to be a dog, but that was the only explanation of why a feral animal will be on the streets. He looked like he had been in a very rough fight with a dog or more. His fur was knotted with dried blood, and his eyes were bloodshot but bright. Jessie took a step further and stretched out her hand. With a snarl and flash of teeth, the dog recoiled and backed away.

"That was strange," Jessie muttered to herself. She was usually good with animals, but it seemed the wounded dog didn't trust anyone. She sighed and walked to the comfort of her home.

As she opened the worn-out gate leading to the apartment building, the loud atmosphere hit Jessie. The apartment building was home to families with noisy children, a wife who wouldn't stop yelling, a rock band member who felt the need to practice at home, loudly, every day, and a combination of people with chaotic and rowdy lives.

Jessie stared at the broken-down elevator and sighed in exasperation. This was the third time it would be breaking down, and she had to take the long flight of stairs. Finally, she got to her room and looked around with relief. She had had a long day, and the quaint but cozy comfort of her home put her at ease. In the residence, there were two rooms, one which she used as a living room and the second which was her bedroom. The lilac wallpaper added some cheer to the otherwise dark room, and Jessie turned on the switch to light her room. There was a large sofa in the middle of the room, and it was Jessie's favorite and only furniture in her living room. She got it as a gift from her mother when she turned 27, right before her health began to decline.

Jessie walked into the bathroom and filled the bathtub with water. She threw in her favorite strawberry-scented bath bomb and stripped. Jessie sank into the warm water and let out a soft sigh of relief. She allowed herself to soak for much longer than usual but finally came out when she started feeling cold.

Jessie grabbed a large fluffy towel and wrapped herself in it. She didn't feel sleepy yet, so she wore her Peppa pig pajamas and sat in front of her small flat-screen TV. She went through various channels before settling on an old cowboy movie.

Jessie dragged herself from the couch and decided to find something to quiet the hungry growl of her stomach. She opened her fridge and was glad to find leftover pasta. She popped it into the microwave and pulled out her phone till the timer went off.

"I lost my job." Aimee was her former roommate, and the only friend Jessie had had in a while. Aimee moved out when she found a marketing job in California.

A phone call immediately came in, and Jessie didn't have to check if it was Aimee.

"Oh my god, what happened?"

Jessie gave her a quick rundown of what had happened, and she felt the emotions come back to her.

"Jess, you can come here. You can move in with me, and we'll find you a job."

Jessie smiled at the kind gesture. This was why she missed Aimee. "I can't leave mom. I'll find something to do."

The timer went off, and Jessie decided to hang up. "Hey, I'll talk to you later."

"Oh, okay. I'll call you tomorrow. We'll find a solution."

They said their goodbyes, and Jessie grabbed her pasta and sat on the chair.

She could no longer concentrate on the movie she was watching, so she turned the TV off. She sat on her blue sofa, holding her plate of pasta, and for the first time, she realized what losing her job would mean for herself and her mother. For the first time all day, Jessie allowed herself to cry. Finally, she sank into a dreamless and restless sleep.

Chapter 2

The smell of bleach and antiseptics that was always particular to hospitals felt like it was hanging on to Jessie's clothes. In the six months that she had been frequenting the hospital, she still couldn't get herself to be familiar with the strong smell.

Jessie shuffled her feet, and she sat in the waiting room. She was a familiar face, and she could easily skip the line, but she always chose to stay with the rest of the visitors. After all, everyone else had their reasons for being here.

"Jessie Lewis, you can come up now." Mandy, the nurse at the front desk, smiled and beckoned to her.

Jessie walked up to her and gave her a genuine smile. "Hey, how are you?"

Mandy was a robust woman who always looked flustered. Jessie thought she was huggable and seemed like a sweet older woman. "Oh, you know, just doing my thing. By the way, Devon won the first prize in his third-grade poetry competition! I'm so proud of him! We're coming to the shop to celebrate."

Jessie felt her heart drop. Mandy and her only son, Devon, frequented the coffee shop and were regular customers. Jessie cleared her throat. "The shop... we shut it down. Yesterday."

Mandy's eyes widened as she gasped, "Why? What happened?"

"The shop is in bankruptcy. Jerry couldn't afford to keep it floating anymore. "

Mandy looked at her with pity and put her hands on top of Jessie's in the way of showing comfort. "If you want anything, let me know, please."

"Thank you, Mandy. Let me check on Ma."

Jessie walked down the corridor and looked at the familiar doors. In the six months she had been there, her mother had had four different neighbors, and the recent one was a little boy diagnosed with Leukemia. That didn't affect his cheerful attitude regardless. She wasn't sure what his name was, but she called him Billy in her head, simply because he looked like a Billy.

Jessie looked into the shielded window and waved at him. He seemed to be playing a game, but he dropped the tablet and waved back at her.

He seems to be looking better, Jessie thought.

She knocked on the door that housed her mother and entered when she heard a muffled 'come in.'

Jessie squinted to adjust to the darkness of the room. It was 9 am, but the curtains were shut, and the lights were off. The white walls looked drab in the darkness, and so did the blue-colored floor tiles. Jessie walked to the window and pulled the curtains apart, bathing the room with natural light.

"Jessie! Are you trying to burn my eyes?" Hannah Lewis stared at her daughter with annoyance while trying to adjust to the sudden brightness. She tried to sit up, but that seemed to take a lot of effort, so she just lay on the sterile white bed sheets with blue blankets.

Jessie rolled her eyes and leaned in to kiss her mother on the cheeks. Her formerly soft and robust cheeks were now sunken, and the skin felt harsh to the touch. Jessie decided not to point that out. Her mother was already self-conscious about losing weight.

Hannah scowled, but Jessie could see the sparkle in her eyes. Her mother had missed her. Her hair had to be shaved by the surgeons to conduct a head surgery, but it had overgrown. Hannah's dark hair was already forming into a pixie cut, and she hoped they wouldn't have to shave it again.

Jessie handed over the bag she had been holding over to Hannah. "I got you some strawberries."

Hannah smiled genuinely and grabbed the bag. She opened the Tupperware and pulled out a moist and fresh strawberry fruit.

"How are you feeling?"

Hannah shrugged her bony shoulders as she munched on the strawberries. "The doctors said they might need to perform another test on me. Not sure what for."

Jessie made a mental note to talk to the doctor in charge of her mother. They settled into a familiar silence, only interrupted by healthcare workers' soft footsteps going up and down the hallway.

They had always been like this, staying together in silence while acknowledging each other's silence. Jessie never knew her father, and every time she asked about him, her mother would say, "He doesn't deserve to be in your life. Trust me, you can live without him."

And that was what she did. Jessie grew up in a small community before settling down in Albany. Jessie had had her share of 'father figures,' like the lovely but weird schoolteacher her mother had dated when she was 17, the architect she married when Jessie was 21. The marriage only lasted for two years before he decided Hannah was too eccentric for him.

Hannah had worked a couple of odd jobs before she became a secretary at a small publishing country. She resigned when her coworker found her passed out on the restroom floor.

"How's work?" The silence that followed Hannah's question begged to be filled by anything just to take the awkwardness away.

Jessie had always found it difficult to lie when she made eye contact, so she looked down at her black boots and answered, "Oh um, it's fine. Yeah."

"That's good. I hope that man gives you a raise for all the work you've been doing. You need to buy some skincare products for yourself. Your skin looks so dry, and those eye bags need to go."

"Mom!" Jessie surprised both herself and her mother with the sudden harsh tone in her voice, but she continued. "I can't spend money on trivial things like that. We have to pay the medical bills. I'm pretty sure the skincare can wait."

Hannah's smile faded away as she opened and closed her mouth. "Jessie I... I'm sorry. I was just trying to make something light out of it. You seem really stressed, and I wanted to cheer you up."

Jessie's heart clenched with sadness when she saw the tears forming in Hannah's eyes. She slid into the tiny space beside her and folded into her embrace. For the first time in a while, Jessie felt like she was 10 again, terrified to sleep alone when the rain pounded hard on their tiny house.

"I'm sorry mum. Please don't cry. I promise to get a face cleanser or face mask. I'll even go to the spa. Whatever makes you happy?"

Hannah let out a shaky laugh and ran her hand through Jessie's hair. "It's okay. I understand, and I love you."

"Love you, too, mom."

Even though it was still morning, the mother and daughter soon drifted into a short sleep induced by the monotony beeping of the heart monitor machine.

"Jessie, it is time to leave." Jessie sat up as a tap on the shoulder woke her from her short but sweet sleep. It was Mina, a nurse that Jessie had also gotten familiar with.

"Hey, Mina, sorry about that. I should go." Jessie turned to look at her mother, peacefully sleeping, and she gave her a soft kiss on her cheek before standing up.

Mina smiled and checked the drip connected to Hannah's hand. "It's alright. Visiting hours are over. Plus, you don't want to wake her up. She has been finding it a bit difficult to fall asleep naturally. This is quite a surprise to see her peaceful sleeping with no drugs or injection."

"Really? Well, I'm glad she is finally asleep. Let me know if anything more comes up please."

"Of course. Have a good day."

Jessie walked out of the room, and Mina shut the door softly. They were walking down the corridor together when Mina cleared her throat to speak.

"I'm sorry about what happened with the coffee shop. It must be hard for you."

Jessie felt her face turn red. Either she had found out on her own, or Hannah had told her. Regardless of how Mina had gotten to know, Jessie felt embarrassed.

Mina noticed Jessie's face turn red and quickly rushed to reassure her. "Oh no, no, don't feel bad. It's not your fault in any way. I'll be sending something I think you may want to look into. What's your email?"

Mina handed Jessie her cellphone, and Jessie quickly typed in her email.

Jessie muttered, "Thank you very much."

"Sure, it's nothing. Oh, I almost forgot! Doctor Lucas wants to see you."

Jessie's heart hammered as she ran through different reasons why the doctor in charge of her mother wanted to see her. Was she getting worse?

"Why? What for?"

"I'm sorry, I don't know."

Jessie nodded and absentmindedly waved goodbye to Mina. Although Doctor Lucas's office was on another floor, the distance wasn't a lot, and soon, Jessie lingered in front of the office, still wondering what it could be.

Finally, she knocked and opened the door.

Doctor Lucas had always been a stern-looking man, and he always seemed to have a sneer on his face. But for whatever reason, most patients preferred for him to be their doctor. Jessie assumed he was nicer to sick people.

"Miss Lewis, please take a seat."

Jessie sank into the rigid leather chair across him and looked everywhere but his eyes. He always seemed to make her feel uncomfortable anytime they had their brief meetings.

Doctor Lucas adjusted his glasses and stared at Jessie for a while before opening his mouth to speak. "After this test we are about to conduct on your mother, I'm sorry, but we won't be able to go further until you pay the medical bills, which are already due."

Jessie felt her throat seize. What? How can this happen now?

"Please, there must be something we can work out. I just lost my job and-"

"I'm sorry, Miss Lewis, but this isn't something in my control. Please have a nice day."

The conversation was over, and Jessie took the hint. She stood on shaky legs and walked out of the office. Jessie couldn't take a loan because she had no collateral. She stepped out the door and deeply breathed in the warm air. She felt her head spinning and took a quick seat on a nearby bench. She didn't want to think about any of that, so she allowed herself to be distracted by the soothing voice of a man singing to the rhythm of a ukulele.

Her phone chimed as a notification box popped up. It was an email from Minasanderson01. Jessie remembered that Mina had promised to send something to her.

She opened the message and read it loudly to herself. "Hey! It's Mina. Check out this link. I think you will want to consider this."

Jessie stared at the link at the end of the text. It seemed to be for a job search site, and Jessie wasn't sure about that. She never really went to college because they couldn't afford it, and when she decided to go, her mother had fallen sick.

Realizing she might as well try, she opened the link. It was the only message there, so she didn't miss it.

'We are looking for a home keeper who will be available six times a week. They must take care of the cleaning and laundry and may have to perform miscellaneous duties when required. During your stay, nothing must go missing or you will be responsible for the cost. Please call this number if you are interested.'

Jessie stared at the number. It all looked too simple and straightforward. She scowled down a bit and realized the salary was there. She felt her throat seize up as she looked at the glaring number on the screen. Jessie stood up in such haste that the birds peacefully picking up pieces of bread flew away.

How does a cleaner get this much? And why is the position not taken yet?

Jessie rubbed her eyes and looked at the number again; to make sure what she was seeing was real. $30,000 per month.

She sat down and scrolled down the rest of the page. There was a column for reviews, so she opened it.

Adele2011: It's horrible! The pay is a lot, but I couldn't take it anymore. I wouldn't recommend anyone taking this. It is not worth it.

Wendyattaway24: I had to quit because I was crying every day. Such hurtful words.

"LisacowellNY: I had to stay over one night and had nightmares. Strange things are going on in that house. I didn't last a month."

There were more reviews like these, and they were all complaints. Jessie felt discouraged and nervous. Why were the reviews so bad? And how many people had been fired in the last month? From what she could see, four different people had already worked there in the month.

But then, $30,000? She had handled spoilt brats and snotty adults; it couldn't be that difficult anyway.

Jessie typed the number on her phone and dialed it. After two rings, someone picked up.

"Irving mansion. How may I help you?" A cheerful voice sounded through the phone, and Jessie felt relieved. Whoever it was, they sounded happy enough.

"Um, hi. I saw your ad and would like to apply."

The person hesitated, "Are you sure?"

Jessie was taken aback as to why she would try to discourage her from taking the job. It didn't matter anyway; she was going to seize the one in a million opportunity.

"Yes, I do."

"Alright then! I'm Amelia. I will be sending the address to you. I'm assuming this is your phone number! If it is not, please forward your private line."

"It is, this is my phone number." Jessie fumbled with her tote bag and hurriedly pulled out a small notebook and a pencil.

"Oh, great then. Please, arrive on time. Enjoy your day Miss..."

Jessie rushed to reply, "Jessie Lewis."

" Alright then, see you tomorrow Miss Lewis." Then, the phone went off. Jessie sat back on the park bench and processed what to say.

I have never been a housekeeper before, but I'm sure it's cleaning. I did a lot of that at the coffee shop, she thought.

Jessie checked the time on her phone and saw that it was a few hours past noon. For the very first time in years, she had a free weekday, and she wasn't sure what to do with it. She turned to look at the park and found the scenery calming. It was May, and the trees' green hue seemed to add some cheer to the weather. A mom and her two kids were running around, playing with their dog and blowing bubbles. The sun on Jessie's neck felt surprisingly welcoming. She was enjoying the serenity and carefree nature of the outdoors.

The faint yet high-pitched laughter of children was mixed with the barks of dogs. She realized not everyone spends their weekdays cooped in a coffee shop, trying to clean and serve at the same time.

A high-pitched whine interrupted Jessie's thoughts. The dog that the kids had been running after was lying on the grass. Jessie stood up and slowly walked up to them as their mother came running.

She looked at Jessie with suspicion. "How can I help you?"

At 5'6 ft, Jessie didn't think she was considered tall, but she had good inches over the 5ft dwarf staring her down. The lady was dressed in a blue cashmere turtleneck and dark jeans paired with white sneakers. Her auburn-colored hair was drawn into a messy bun on top of her head. Jessie looked at her two children. The boy was about seven years old and had his mom's hair. He scowled at her, probably wondering what Jessie wanted. The five-year-old girl was kneeling beside the dog, crying. She had beautiful dark hair, and when she turned to look up at Jessie, she could see that she had bright blue eyes like her mother.

Jessie ignored the lady and knelt behind the dog. It was a male Siberian husky, and Jessie could see that his left hind limb seemed to be the problem. She softly touched the swollen part, and the husky let out a yelp.

"You're hurting him!"

Jessie shook her head. "He is already hurt. It seems like he dislocated his limb. You will have to take him to the vet."

The red-haired woman threw her hands up, "We can't afford a vet, especially not now."

The little girl cried harder, and Jessie's heart broke a little.

"Okay, there's another solution. But this might hurt him a little."

The little girl nodded her head frantically, "I just want Bobo to be okay."

Jessie felt a laugh rise out of her, but she quickly turned it into a cough. Who named a Siberian husky 'Bobo'?

Jessie sat down on the grass and tried to put the dog on her lap. It growled at her as he had never seen her before.

"It's okay," Jessie said in a soothing voice. "I'm not going to hurt you."

Bobo let out a little whine but allowed him to be carried. Jessie gently pulled out the limp leg and rubbed his back as he howled in pain. She tenderly pulled it straight and quickly popped the bone back in place before he could register the pain. Bobo let out a loud screech before settling into a whimper.

Jessie turned to look at the mom, who was staring at her with wonder. "It's still tender, but his bone is back in place. You will have to restrict his movement for some time. Don't worry; his leg will heal properly in no time."

The little girl stood up to hug her, her tiny arms going around Jessie's neck. "Thank you so much."

Jessie smiled awkwardly at her. While the little girl was adorable, Jessie didn't have much experience with kids as she grew up to be the only child of her mother. A look of admiration replaced the boy's scowl. Although he didn't mention it, Jessie could see that he was grateful.

"Oh my, thank you! What would we have done? Forgive my manners, I'm Lucy Hale."

"Of course, anything to help. I'm Jessie Lewis." She couldn't help but ruefully think that this was the second time she would be introducing herself twice in one afternoon. That didn't happen often.

"Kids, introduce yourselves." Lucy raised her brows at her children.

The little girl seemed to be the friendlier one, so she spoke first. "My name is Mia Hale, and I love bubbles and SpongeBob!" The enthusiasm in her voice was catchy, and Jessie was surprised when she giggled at Mia's excitement.

The boy cleared his throat. For a seven-year-old, he looked serious for his age. "My name is Aaron."

It seemed like that was all Jessie would be getting from him, so she nodded in response. She picked up the dog and carried him in her arms. Bobo seemed to have warmed up to her as he softly rubbed his head against Jessie's sleeve.

She turned to look at Lucy. "Do you have a car? He shouldn't walk for now."

"Oh yes, right this way." Lucy quickly went to grab their picnic basket and the mat she had spread on the ground. Jessie felt sorry that their picnic had to be cut short. They seemed to have been having a lot of fun.

Slowly, the little party walked to a parking lot where their car stood. It was a 2004 Toyota SUV that seemed to have encountered a lot. Lucy threw the things they used for the picnic into the backseat and beckoned to the children.

"Come on guys, time to go. I need to get you secured to your seats." Mia climbed into her booster seat, and Lucy made sure it was keyed correctly. Although Aaron didn't need a booster seat, Lucy made him put his safety belt on and keep it locked. Jessie couldn't help but admire how she seemed to have settled into this routine.

Jessie set down Bobo carefully onto the backseat. He whined as he turned to leave, so Jessie gave him a soft kiss on his head.

She had turned to leave when Lucy abruptly stopped her. "Oh, there's no way you are leaving just like that. Please join us for lunch."

"No, it's fine. I'm heading home, so I'll-"

Lucy shook her head; some strands of her hair fell out of her bun. "There is no way I'm taking no for an answer. Plus, we are going to Burger King."

Just on time, Jessie's stomach growled. Lucy raised her eyebrows at the sound in an I-told-you-so manner.

Jessie shrugged and hopped into the passenger seat of the vehicle. It was free food anyway. Lucy started the engine, and they revved out of the parking lot.

The car moved slowly, and Jessie couldn't help but think, why is she driving so slowly? There were hardly any vehicle on the road.

As if reading her thoughts, Lucy smiled sheepishly at her, "I'm sorry. I always drive like this. I've tried, but I can't drive fast. Maybe it's an irrational fear for Mia and Aaron."

"Oh no, your fear isn't irrational. Drive the way you feel comfortable with. It's perfectly fine."

Satisfied with her answer, Lucy nodded and smiled, turning to focus on the road.

A popular kiddie's song started playing on the radio, and Mia started singing along and bounced to it. Jessie turned to grin at her. She was such a happy child.

A few minutes later, they drove into the driveway of a nearby Burger King shop.

"Okay, guys, down! Down! Let's move." Lucy unbuckled their seatbelts and helped them down. Jessie watched all of it happen in few seconds. She was impressed as to how she quickly handled the two kids all by herself.

Bobo whimpered when he realized he would be left alone in the car. Mia leaned into him and hugged him. "I'll bring you some chicken, Bobo. I promise."

Bobo seemed comforted by that, so he closed his eyes and went to sleep. They all walked into the fast-food restaurant, and Jessie was surprised to see the place packed up, even though it was about 2 pm. At Jerry's, their busy hours were usually in the morning or later in the evening. Afternoons were always slow; Jessie imagined it was the same everywhere.

"What will you get?" Lucy clapped her hands and looked at them with wide eyes. Jessie stared at her in awe. How was so much energy contained in such a small frame?

Mia, as expected, spoke first. "I want a double cheeseburger and chicken nuggets."

Lucy ruffled her hair, "Hungry today, aren't we? Aaron?"

Aaron had been so quiet that Jessie almost forgot he was there. She really hoped he would loosen up a bit.

"A Crispy chicken sandwich and a soft vanilla serve."

Lucy nodded and turned to Jessie, "What about you?"

"No, it's okay. I can just order myself and-"

Lucy put her hand on her hip. "I already told you, this is just me saying thank you. Now, what would you like?"

Jessie shrugged, defeated. She wasn't used to having people do nice things for her. "I'll have whatever you have."

"Spicy chicken sandwich and a strawberry shake. Sounds good?"

Jessie nodded and gave her a genuine smile. "Sure it does. Thanks again."

Lucy playfully rolled her eyes. "You just might thank me to death. It is nothing. I'll be back. Kids, behave."

Mia reached out to touch Jessie's hair. "I love your hair. It's so shiny." Jessie giggled and put a hand to her hair. To save money, she stopped taking expensive haircuts and decided to go with the neck-length hairstyle. It was basic, but it felt nice that someone else noticed.

Lucy came back to her seat and clapped her hands, "So our meals are on the way. Jessie, how did you know what to do about Bobo?"

Jessie scratched her neck awkwardly; telling this story always made her sound like a strange person. "As a child, my mom went out a lot - to work, of course - and we had a vet doctor who had his small clinic right next to us. Most times, my mom would drop me off with him, and I'll help out. I ended up picking a lot from him until we moved."

Lucy nodded as she listened. She looked impressed, and Jessie felt a surge of pride flow through her.

The server brought their meals and the mood around the table lifted. Even Aaron became more vocal and talked about the ongoing science project in his school.

"Oh! Jessie, I should give you my number. We recently moved here, and lord knows I could use a friend."

"Of course, sure." Jessie handed Lucy her phone, and she typed her number into it.

As the sunset into a golden yellow and laughter resonated around the table, Jessie couldn't help but deliberate about how it will be like to eventually have a friend.

Chapter 3

Jessie woke up to sunlight filtering through her curtains, casting a golden hue on her bedroom. It reminded her of the time she and her mother went to spend a week in Rwanda as a way to celebrate her 18th birthday.

For a moment, Jessie conjured the images of the waves slowly washing onto the beach, the sun tenderly tanning her skin, and she gently let go of the memory. A new day had begun, and she had to prepare for her interview at 9 pm. Jessie got up from her bed and walked up to the curtain. She pulled it apart only to see another apartment building facing her window.

"Way to ruin the mood," she scoffed and walked to the bathroom. Jessie turned the tap, and nothing came out.

"What is this?" She vigorously turned the head of the tap, but nothing came out. Her jaw fell open. He wouldn't do that, would he? The dratted old man!

Jessie hurriedly wore her flip-flops and threw a jacket over her pajamas. She marched downstairs and knocked hard on the first door to the left.

The door opened, and the landlord, Jeff, stood in the doorway. His beefy body filled the entire frame, and his frown changed to a smirk when he saw it was Jessie.

"Ah, I see you have gotten the message."

Jessie gritted her teeth in frustration. "What message? Why did you turn off the water?"

He crossed his arms and shrugged; the fat in his arms quivered with the action. "Until you pay your rent."

Jessie lost it. *Are you kidding me? I have to get ready for an interview in less than an hour and you decide to lock my water off because rent that's only three days late? Are you freaking kidding me?"*

The other residents came out to see what was going on, and murmurs passed between them. Soon, they were all scowling at Jeff. He shifted uncomfortably under the scrutiny but maintained his stand.

"Well, you have to pay before-"

Jessie narrowed her eyes. "I swear, Jeff, if you do not turn my water on, I promise I will tell."

Jeff turned beet red, and his eye widened in horror. Some weeks before, Jessie had come back late and walked in on Jeff running around in a tiny batman costume while high as a kite.

He wordlessly walked out of the room and down the stairs to turn on her water.

"Way to go, Jess!" Mr. Billy, a carpenter, clapped with an impressed look on his face. Her other neighbors started cheering and clapping.

"Finally, someone to stand up to that bully."

"Girl, what do you have on him?"

"That was awesome!"

Jessie couldn't help but grin at them all. "Thank you, guys. I have to go or I'll be late."

'Good luck' and 'you got this' rang through the air as they all walked back to their respective apartments. Jessie hurried to hers and got the quickest shower ever. She picked out her best outfit; a button-down pale blue shirt with dark slacks. Jessie pulled out her favorite Doc Martins boots and paired them with her lucky SpongeBob socks.

She had never been a huge fan of makeup, but she wanted to look more formal than usual, so she dabbed on a little foundation and applied strawberry-flavored gloss on her lips. When it was 20 minutes to the scheduled time, Jessie finally locked her room and set out for the day.

It was a regular Tuesday in Albany, and everyone walked by each other hurriedly without paying attention to the people around them. Teenagers rode their skateboards on the sidewalks, almost bumping into the businessmen that always seemed to be on a call or the other.

Cars raced by and only slowed down when the lights turned red. They all seemed to be in a hurry and oblivious to everything else around them. I was once like this, rushing to the coffee shop right before we opened for the day, Jessie thought.

Luckily for her, it didn't take too long for a bus to come to a pause at the stop. She wasn't sure she had ever boarded any bus going to Cleveland Avenue, where the Irving mansion was, but she decided to ask the driver.

She climbed in and asked, "Hi. I was wondering, will this get to Cleveland Avenue?"

The bus driver looked like she was insane. "Yaw, ain't nobody been to that side ever since dem strange things started happening. But I can get you close enough."

Jessie didn't have the time to ask more questions because the bus got full and started moving. She had taken a seat by the window and was looking out of it. Her mind could only think of one thing. What strange things, and why hadn't she heard about them till this moment? She shook the thoughts from her head; it was probably something silly anyway.

Surprisingly, the journey was short, and the bus stopped at Addison Avenue, close to Cleveland Avenue.

"Thank you."

The driver nodded with a sober look on his face. "Be careful. That place gives me the creeps. Never gone too close, though."

Jessie nodded but pushed it away from her mind. She wasn't going to let anyone scare her. The bus drove away, and she was alone in a quiet neighborhood. She looked at the time on her phone, and there were only ten minutes left.

"Crap," Jessie said and began to walk fast. The driver had told her Cleveland Avenue was straight ahead, so getting there wouldn't be so hard. Her once damp hair was now frizzy, and Jessie tried to smoothen it down. She saw few people on the way, and most of them were in front of their homes, trying to sort some things.

All of a sudden, Jessie came to a stop in front of a forest. There was no way anything went beyond that. The forest looked dense, and it seemed weird that there was a thicket of the bush right in front of an entire neighborhood. She looked behind her, but it was only the rest of Addison Avenue; going forward was the only way.

She took a deep breath and plunged into the forest. Luckily, sunlight pierced through the thick trees, and the place looked bright enough. There was a clear narrow path that indicated the path was frequently used, putting Jessie at ease. The forest was eerily quiet, and there was the occasional cawing of birds. Jessie started humming the tune of a catchy song to keep her imagination from running wild, and she briskly walked.

Eventually, the trees thinned out, and Jessie burst into a cleared and empty space. She shielded her eyes from the sun and looked at the looming object that cast a shadow on her. It was a house. The biggest apartment she had ever seen in her life.

"Oh my gosh. This can't be real." But in fact, it was real. It was right in front of her. Her phone beeped as the alarm she had set went off. It was 9 am already. Jessie quickly ran to the looming gate in front of the mansion. Although the house had the architecture of a colossal mansion, Jessie noticed the state-of-the-art intercom. She wasn't sure what to press, so she stared at it for seconds, wondering what to press.

Unexpectedly, a buzz sounded from the speaker, and a robotic voice spoke next. Miss Lewis, welcome to the Irving Mansion. The gates will open in 3, 2,1..."

Jessie watched in awe as a small passenger gate that she hadn't even noticed opened. She quickly walked in through the gate and tried to smoothen her already wrinkled shirt. As much as she tried to keep herself composed, Jessie stared at the house in awe as she walked to the mansion. Right in the middle of the extended driveway was a gold fountain that had the statue of Artemis spewing clear water from her mouth.

The house itself stretched so Jessie had to crane her neck to see all of it. Finally, she stood in front of the towering mahogany door. As she was about to knock, the door slowly opened by itself.

Jessie wondered what she must look like, with her jaw almost hanging on the floor, but with what she was looking at, she couldn't help herself.

While the mansion already looked huge from the outside, the interior architecture was much more overwhelming. The middle of the hallway was a large marble staircase that led to the house's numerous rooms and spaces.

The walls were painted the walls saint white, and it seemed the predominant colors were white and darker hues. Jessie walked slightly further and noticed a few windows in the hallway, but a gigantic glass chandelier provided enough light that everything looked washed in natural lights.

The clanking of heels could be heard coming down the stairs, and Jessie quickly composed herself. She was tempted to remove her muddy boots because staining the bright white floor tiles seemed like a sin. A tall woman who seemed to be glowing walked down the stairs, gingerly holding the silver railings.

Her cheekbones were high and protruding and even more accentuated by her nude makeup on her face. Her blond hair was pulled into a sleek low bun, and she wore a simple yet classy blue dress that stopped at the knees.

She came to a stop in front of Jessie and smiled at her, pearly white teeth gleaming under the light. "Jessie Lewis, it is nice to meet you. I'm Amelia Reyes. Please follow me. "

Jessie walked beside her and struggled to keep up. Even though Amelia was wearing heels, she moved quite fast.

"We will be taking the interview as we tour the house, so do your best to answer adequately."

Jessie nodded, but she felt the wheels in her head-turning. What would she ask?

They walked up the stairs, and it led into another hallway. The lighting in this space was darker as the predominant colors were dark with tan and gold highlights. A beautiful eighteenth-century fireplace was on the wall opposite them, and although the fireplace was unlit, Jessie could see that the ambers were glowing dully, which means it had been put off not long ago.

"So, do you have any experience cleaning homes?" Amelia glanced at Jessie as they came to a pause in the room.

" Err, no." Amelia cocked a brow at her. "But I worked for five years at a coffee shop. I had to clean too." Jessie rushed to answer.

Amelia nodded slowly, and they moved. They halted in front of a tall, heavy-looking oak double doors, and Amelia pushed it open to reveal another hallway. Exactly how many corridors are in this huge house? Jessie thought. She shuddered at the idea of getting lost in one of the hallways.

To the right was a small living room. Another fireplace was situated at the east corner of the room and had a mantel of Birchwood with tiny naked figurines arranged on it. The ceiling was painted a cream color, and a candle chandelier hung from it. The tall French windows had transparent markings on them, and Jessie admired the intricacy of it. The wallpapers were the classic Franco-Japanese with floral and Greek themes on the ceilings and walls.

Amelia stopped to plop a pillow that looked to be out of position. Jessie took the opportunity to scan the room properly. It didn't look lived in. it was very neat, and she wondered if they had a cleaner before her or the owner didn't live in it.

Amelia straightened and crossed her hands behind her back. "As you can see, this is quite a large house, and we have our reasons for choosing just one person to clean the entire space. The question is can you handle it?"

Jessie mentally ran the structure of the house in her mind. From what she had seen so far, there were four floors and probable up to thirty rooms in the house, minus the other spaces she hadn't seen yet. It was a lot, but she didn't have much choice.

"Yes, I can handle it."

"Good. Let's head downstairs." They walked out of the room and back into the hallway. Jessie noticed a center arch of decorative painted pillars with decorative gemstone designs on it.

The dining room was the next stop they came to after climbing down the staircase. There were panel doors on the east wall, and Jessie assumed it led to the pantry or storage. They were headed to the kitchen when Amelia spoke again.

If there was anywhere, Jessie decided she could tag as her favorite place, and it was the kitchen. The walls were painted a light grey, and it balanced adequately with the dark grey cabinets that lined the walls. The counter in the middle was made of shiny white crystallized glass, and high wooden stools were arranged in front of it.

There was a large floor-to-ceiling window that provided a view of the pool at the house's back. There was a stainless steel Miele oven and cooktop on the far west wall.

"Miss Lewis." Amelia brought Jessie back to attention. "Why should we hire you?"

Jessie considered saying this because she was a dedicated worker. While that was true, it wasn't the reason she was taking the job. So, she settled for the truth.

"Because I need the money, and I'm going to work hard to get it."

The silence after this left Jessie's heart pounding. Had she messed things up for herself? Amelia stared at her for seconds, and Jessie had to fight the urge to look away. Instead, she held her gaze.

Finally, Amelia nodded. "Alright. By the way, I'm assuming you know who Seth Irving is?"

Jessie searched her memory for a Seth Irving, but nothing came up. She slowly shook her head. "No, should I?"

Amelia looked at her incredulously. "You have never heard of Seth Irving? What about Flutter Wines?"

Jessie nodded at the familiarity of the name. Who didn't know the largest liquor company in all of the U.S?

"Well, I'm surprised you don't know the CEO is Seth Irving. Do you live under a rock?"

Jessie gasped and put a hand to her mouth. No way was she in the home of one of the youngest billionaires in America.

Amelia chuckled at her reaction. "You do live under a rock. Well, Jessie, our meeting is over, and I still have other people to interview. I will be giving you a call to let you know how it fares. Do have a great day."

Jessie remembered she'd have to go through the forest again, and she frowned.

Amelia noticed. "What's the problem?"

Jessie shook her head. "Nothing... it's just that the forest is a bit creepy and-"

"Wait, did you pass the forest to get here?"

"Well, yes."

Amelia laughed and shook her head. "So you did not see the gate beside the forest? The one that leads to this place?"

Jessie's eyes widened, and she burst into a giggle when she remembered how she struggled to get here. All the while, there had been a gate beside the forest?

"Come, I'll show you." They both walked out of the house, and the gate automatically shut behind them. Amelia stood in front of the mansion and pointed somewhere near the forest. Jessie squinted, and true enough, there was a paved road right beside the forest, which led to a tiny gate.

"Wow, thank you."

"Of course. And you can easily order a taxi from there with no hassle."

Jessie opened her mouth to ask about what the bus driver had said and the fact that there was a small cleared path in the forest, but she changed her mind. It didn't matter.

She waved goodbye to Amelia and watched the gate firmly shut itself behind her. Indeed, Jessie only had to walk for few minutes before getting to the road.

"Taxi!" She waved down a cab as it sped by. The car slowed down, and Jessie pondered on where to go. Again, she realized how boring her life was ever since she stopped working at the coffee shop.

"Take me to No 2 Barne street." She wanted to see Jerry's again. She hadn't been there since the shop closed, and out of curiosity, Jessie wanted to see what the building looked like without its usual flurry of activities.

Jessie sat at the back of the taxi, and it sped away. Luckily, it wasn't so far away, so Jessie didn't have to worry about spending too much. She had to be careful with how she spent, or else she would run out of money.

Finally, the cab came to a stop in front of Jerry's. Jessie paid and got down from the taxi. She wasn't sure what she had been expecting, but it looked almost the same. There was a SHUT DOWN sign posted on the door, and it was all locked, but it was the same. Now that she was here, Jessie didn't know what to do. She could see Hannah, but she didn't want to run into Doctor Lucas. So Jessie stood in front of the coffee shop for five minutes, watching the blurry figures walk past her.

She whipped out her phone and decided to call one person she hoped would be glad to hangout. After two rings, she picked up.

"Hello."

Jessie cleared her throat. "Hey Lucy, it's Jessie. I hope I'm not bothering."

"Oh my, Jess! No, it's fine. How are you?"

"I'm good. Um, I was hoping we could just...maybe hang out? That's if you are free, of course." Jessie felt her face turn red. She sounded like a person with zero friends and no social life.

"I'd love that! Where do you want us to go? The kids are in school, and I'm bored out of my mind."

Jessie racked her head, but nothing came to mind. "How about you pick where we'll go?"

Lucy chuckled. "Well, will you look at that? The woman who just moved here should pick the spot." Even though Lucy was teasing, Jessie's face burned with embarrassment.

She continued, "I have a spot anyway. Where are you?"

"I'm on Barne's street."

"Okay, I'll pick you in ten."

"Awesome! I'll see you then. Bye."

She hung up, and for the first time that day, Jessie gave a genuine smile. I guess I have a new friend, she thought.

Jessie opened her tote bag to put my mobile phone into while walking away from the coffee shop. Her bracelet got hooked with the bag. She was struggling to unhook it when she bumped into a wall.

"Ouch!" Jessie looked up, and the wall turned out to be the hard chest of a tall hooded figure.

"Are you blind?" his deep voice seemed to vibrate through her as a result of their close proximity. Jessie took a step back.

"Oh, I'm sorry. I didn't see you there. I was trying to- "

"If you know you are this clumsy, then don't walk while doing something else."

Jessie frowned at him. She had already apologized; what was he rude for? "Excuse me? I already apologized. What's your problem?"

His hood was on, and she could barely see his eyes beneath the dark shades he was wearing, but Jessie saw his eyebrows shoot up with surprise.

"My problem? You are the one who crash into me."

"And I apologized. Stop walking around with a stick up your ass."

The stranger spat, and Jessie could see a storm brewing up, so she just walked away. She only walked few feet ahead before turning back to look. He was gone.

"Well, good riddance." She rested against the wall and waited for Lucy to arrive. Five minutes later, her familiar car pulled up, and there was her new friend, grinning in the drivers' seat.

"Hey, get in!" Jessie felt her mood lighten up, and she opened the door and sat beside her.

Lucy looked at her with concern. "Are you okay? You seem strained."

Jessie sighed, "I've had a long morning. Plus, I had a run-in with some asshole."

Lucy tsk-tsked. "Well, let's make you feel better. There's this lovely tea shop not too far from here. I have a feeling you'll love it." She turned the car on, and the engine roared as Lucy sped. Jessie stared at her with surprise written all over her face. She had two kids yet was filled with more energy than her.

A famous pop song started playing on the radio, and Lucy sang along at the top of her voice.

Jessie giggled, and Lucy looked at her. "Oh my gosh, I love this song. Sing with me."

Jessie shrugged and started singing the lyrics at the top of her voice." Some people want it all, But I don't want nothing at all, if it ain't you baby if I ain't got, you baby."

Lucy laughed and clapped her hands. "So, you can sing! Nice! Hey, we are here already."

It was an outdoor tea shop, and there were tables and chairs right outside the building. The canopy fluttered as a light breeze blew through it, and chatters and soft laughs filled the air.

They sat down at a table close to the entrance, and a waitress came up to them.

"Hello, welcome, Sweet Leaves. What will you like to have?"

Lucy picked up the menu and squinted at it. "Umm, I want the red rooibos with a scone. Jess? What do you want?"

Jessie picked up the menu in front of her and settled on hibiscus tea and biscuits. The atmosphere was soothing, and her body loosened up.

"So, what's up with you?" Lucy asked her.

"I went for a job interview."

Lucy sat up, a look of anticipation on her face. "How did that go?"

Jessie sighed and shrugged. "I'm not sure. I guess I'll keep looking."

"Aw dang. I'm sure you'll find something. We moved here because of my new job. I'm not resuming till next week anyway. Lord knows I'll need someone to take care of Aaron and Mia when I'm at work."

"Oh? What do you do?"

Lucy had a proud look on her face, and it was clear she loved her job. "I'm a nurse. Will be working at St James hospital."

"Wow, that's amazing. St James is a top-rated hospital. I love that."

The waitress interrupted their conversation and brought them their orders. "Here you go. Enjoy your brunch."

"Thank you." They both said to the lady. Lucy turned to Jessie with concern. "I'm don't know if this is the right thing to ask, but what kind of job are you looking for?"

Jessie shuffled uncomfortably in her seat, but she decided to answer. "Anything that doesn't require a degree. I didn't have the opportunity to go to college. "

"Oh no. I am so sorry."

"Jessie didn't know why, but she felt like opening up, and she did. She hadn't had anyone to talk to in such a long time that it felt relieving to speak to someone. "When I completed high school, I made up my mind to enroll in community college while working, but this didn't turn out well. I dropped out of the college and got a job working at a pizza restaurant in Georgia. My mom and I moved here when I was 23. Two years later, I decided to enroll in art school; I've been painting since I was a little kid. Then my mom got diagnosed with hepatic encephalopathy, and... it has been hard, to say the least."

Lucy held her hand as a way of comforting her. "Oh, darling. I am so sorry. All that pressure on you must be so hard."

Jessie nodded. "It's a lot, but I'll deal."

Lucy sipped her tea and stared into the open space. She had a faraway look on her face and seemed to be remembering something.

"When I was 22, I got married and had Aaron when I was about 24. My ex-husband never allowed me to work because he didn't see any need for it. I enrolled in an online school secretly, and when he went to work, I attended my classes until I bagged a degree in nursing. We got divorced recently, and this job offer was a fresh start for my kids and me."

Jessie looked at Lucy with fresh eyes. She had always seen her as a free spirit with no care in the world. But now that she heard her story, she admired her greatly for being strong.

Jessie raised her teacup. "Well, cheers to that."

Lucy giggled and clanked her cup against Jessie's. "Cheers!"

They sipped their tea, and Lucy told funny stories about Mia and Aaron. Jessie listened to Lucy telling a story about how Aaron had pranked Mia for the last Halloween when her phone rang.

"Sorry, give me a second." She stood up from the table and walked a few feet from there. It was Amelia.

What is she calling me for? Jessie thought as her heart raced. Was she getting an early rejection? She decided to pick up.

"Hello?"

"HI, Jessie. I just want to inform you that you got the job. Congratulations!" The silence that followed was a result of Jessie processing her words.

Had she won? Wait, she got the job!

"Wow, thank you so much! I- wow. I cannot believe it."

"Of course. It's quite interesting, though. Mr. Irving went through all the profiles and decided on yours. I must say, you are lucky."

Jessie turned around to look at Lucy, who had a curious look on her face. She gave her a huge smile and the thumbs-up sign. Lucy clapped and threw her hands in the air.

"Indeed, I am."

"You are free to resume from now till next week. When will you like to begin?"

"Can I start tomorrow?"

Amelia laughed. "Enthusiastic, I see? Anyway, that's not a problem. Come around tomorrow, and I'll be briefing you on all there is to know. "

"Thank you. I'll be there by 9 am. Bye."

Jessie hung up and walked up to a grinning Lucy. "You got the job, didn't you?"

Jessie nodded eagerly, "I did!"

"That's amazing! I love that for you. Congratulations."

"Thank you." Jessie couldn't hold back her happiness, so she laughed out loud. Her life was going to change.

Chapter 4

At fifteen minutes past eight, Jessie was already awake. She flung open her bedroom window and tilted her face to the early-morning sky, and inhaled the cool, fresh air. For the first time in a long time, she appreciated the beauty of nature. Although she couldn't see much as the large building beside her obstructed the view, Jessie imagined skyscrapers peeping into the thick fluffy clouds. That wasn't uncommon in Albany, New York.

She took her time in the shower, much more than she usually did when rushing to the coffee shop, and even used a strawberry-scented bath bomb. Taking a dollop of shampoo, she massaged her hair with the sweet-smelling liquid and rinsed it out with warm water. She brought out her barely used hairdryer and dried her hair. She wasn't sure of what to do with her bobbed hair, so she just combed it down and added a jeweled pin to the side parting.

Jessie brought out her small makeup box and applied nude eyeshadow, blush, and her favorite lip gloss. The weather was warm, so she picked out a sky blue silk blouse and black jeans paired with grey suede flats. She looked into the mirror and could see that she looked like the mature 30-year-old woman she really was. It didn't matter that she would become a cleaner; she would still earn $30,000 per month.

Jessie paused to think about the whole situation, "Why on earth would a cleaner earn 30 grand in a month? Some make that in an entire year." Still, she didn't have an answer, so she made a mental note to ask Amelia; why the salary was that high.

She grabbed her purse and locked the door behind her.

"I see you got the job." It was Jeff. Jessie shuddered at his sudden presence. She hadn't even seen him arrive.

"How did you know that Jeff?"

He rolled his eyes, "Like you dress that nicely every day."

Jessie refused to allow herself to feel offended by his statement, so she just frowned at him.

"You better be paying that rent soon."

Jessie crossed her arms and gave him a fake smile. "Of course I will. Now, I have to go, or I'll be late for my job."

Jeff moved his heavy frame out of the way, and Lucy held her breath as she passed by him. He always stank of fish sticks and engine oil.

Jessie walked into the streets and turned to look at the house she had been living in for the past four years. Why hadn't she noticed how... old it was? The house walls were cracked, and the paint was chipping off. The window shutters looked musky from the outside, and some were even hanging from their hinges.

"Can't wait for mom to get better, and we'll get out of here." Jessie could see it. She and Hannah, lying on a beach in Italy. Jessie shook her head out of the daydream and waved down a taxi. Luckily, the man didn't seem to be concerned about the location, so he dropped her right in front of the gate leading to the Irving mansion.

Jessie smoothed her blouse as she walked the distance to the house. She came halted in front of the vast bronze gate and pushed the intercom button.

The robotic voice sounded. "Miss Lewis, welcome to the Irving Mansion. The gates will open in 3... 2... 1..." and like the last time, the mighty gate swung open, revealing the great house. Like before, the house was eerily silent, and Jessie wondered why the place wasn't overflowing with staff.

"It's not like he can't afford it."

She pushed the doorbell, and the 'dingdong' seemed to resonate throughout the entire house. The door automatically opened, and even though Jessie had only been there once, she wasn't so surprised by the extravagances of the mansion. This time, Amelia was waiting for her in the hallway, a file of papers resting in her arms.

"Jessie! Good morning. How are you today?"

"I'm great. Thank you for this opportunity."

Amelia chuckled and waved her off. "You should thank Mr. Irving, not me."

"You are right. Where is he?"

"Oh, he is in his room. He just arrived yesterday from a business trip, and he is resting a bit. You will get to see him later anyway."

"Alright."

"Please follow me. We'll be going to the study so we can review the contract."

They passed two hallways to get to the study, and on their way there, Jessie tried to get familiar with the hallways and corners. *This will be hard,* she said in her head.

Finally, they arrived at the study. It looked to be more of a library than a study. Books lined the shelves from the ceiling down to the floor. There was an oversized leather couch in the middle of a room, and a window seat was near the Queen Anne's windows, overlooking the city's view. The wooden beams that made up the ceiling were shaped in a triangular way that made the study seem like a house. A shaded chandelier hung from the ceiling and illuminated the room. There was a large oak table with four chairs around it, and that was where they sat.

Amelia opened her files and arranged a couple of papers on the table. She cleared her throat and spoke, "As you know, Mr. Irving is a well-known man, so his business mustn't leave these surroundings. You will be signing a non-disclosure agreement about that. I hope that's okay?"

Jessie sat straight in her seat. "Of course, that is okay. I have no problem with that."

"Awesome. Please sign here." Jessie collected the pen from Amelia and signed where her manicured finger was touching.

She brought out another sheet of paper. "This one is to ensure the transaction between us is valid. You will be paid $30,000 at the end of the month as long as Mr. Irving is satisfied with your work."

Jessie nodded and signed. *He must be satisfied with what I do,* she thought.

The last piece of paper was folded, and when Amelia smoothened it out, it turned out to be a map.

"There are many, many rooms in this house, and I don't want you to get lost, which is why I printed out this map for you. I have clearly labeled the rooms and hallways, so it is easier for you to identify them."

Jessie was touched. "Wow, thank you so much. This is thoughtful."

"It's nothing." Amelia's face got serious. "You are probably the fourth we've employed, and it's just the middle of the month. I am Mr. Irving's assistant, and the only reason you see me here is that the interviews needed to be conducted. I'm not sure why they have all been leaving, but I hope you stay."

"I will work my hardest and make sure I last long enough. The truth is, my mom is sick, and I desperately need the money. I'll endure anything I have to endure."

"Oh, I'm really sorry about that. With the amount of money attached to this, I'm sure you will be able to deal with that?"

Jessie then remembered that she wanted to ask. "Um, I don't know if it's okay to ask, but why is the salary that...much?"

Amelia had a thoughtful look on her face. "Honestly, I don't know. It's quite a lot of money, but Mr. Irving was the one who decided the amount. In fact, it's more than what I earn?"

Jessie's eyes widened with surprise. "A cleaner's earning is more than yours? You're literally in charge."

Amelia shrugged. "If I weren't happy with this job, I would have quitted to become a cleaner myself."

"Wow, that's something."

"Anyway, as for the rooms that are not in use, you don't have to clean them every day. The main rooms to be cleaned often, and I'm talking about the hallways, the living room, the bedrooms, and the kitchen, of course."

"Am I also to cook?" Jessie grimaced at the idea of cooking. She wasn't an excellent cook and survived mainly on takeout and pizza.

"Ooh no, there is a food company that delivers every morning. All you have to do is microwave it if need be. "

"Oh, awesome. So I can start now?"

"Sure! If that's what you want. You are to come six times daily and decide if you want to be paid hourly or at the end of the month. Is that okay with you?"

"It is. I'll rather be paid hourly." Jessie had to pin herself down from jumping up for joy. She could at least pay her rent. Also, she had had to work every day at Jerry's, so it didn't make much of a difference to her.

A loud bang came from upstairs, and it sounded like someone had exited a bedroom.

Amelia clapped her hands. "Oh great, Mr. Irving is awake. It would be best if you introduced yourself. Come on." She stood up, and Jessie followed after her. She straightened the faint wrinkles on her silk blouse as they left the study. She might as well make a good impression on her new boss. They walked down the hallway and into the living room, but he wasn't there.

Amelia looked around. "He is probably in the kitchen."

They walked into the kitchen, and true enough, and a tall, broad man was leaning against the counter, buttering a toast. His back was turned to them, and the hood of his sweater was up so Jessie couldn't see his face. She was dying of curiosity but didn't want to seem rude and forward, so she tilted her head slightly to the ground. Amelia stepped forward, and he turned around at the same time.

He turned around to look at them, and Jessie finally looked up to meet Mariner-blue eyes. He looked Jessie up and down and smirked. His deep voice sent vibrations through her body as he said, "Well, well, nice to meet you again."

Jessie's confusion changed to horror when the voice registered in her head. It was the stranger she had bumped into the day before. "Oh no."

Chapter 5

Jessie stood there, frozen with her jaw slacked and eyes wide open. Amelia looked back and forth at them, confusion on her face.

"Do you know each other?"

Seth Irving sneered at Jessie. "Let's just say; I expect Miss...Jessie to behave herself as long as she is in this house." He put his toast in his mouth and ate it all in one bite. "I hope you will be at least polite to me?"

Jessie composed herself and smiled at him. Even though she felt like screaming about how he was the one who was rude to her, she decided not to do that. "O-of course. I'm sorry about the other time."

He straightened, and Jessie noticed he was much taller than she thought. He waved her off and opened the fridge, bringing out a ham sandwich and orange juice. "Whatever."

He popped the ham sandwich into the microwave and sat down on one of the high stools by the counter. Opening a bag of chips, he downed the orange juice as he ate the chips.

Jessie stared at him with disbelief as he finished the chips as soon as the time went off. She glanced at Amelia and noticed that she was unfazed by it. Who ate that much for breakfast?

As he munched on his sandwich, Jessie was annoyed with herself for noticing how good-looking he was. His dark hair was messy, and few strands stuck to his forehead. He had a five-o'clock shadow, but it barely hid his perfectly chiseled jawline.

His eyebrows were bushy yet perfectly arched, and they were perched over his eyes that had the same color of the ocean. His muscles flexed under the hoodie that did nothing to conceal his fit frame. But Jessie noticed the tremor in his hands and the paleness of the skin. Beads of sweat had gathered on his forehead, and he looked tired.

He turned to catch her looking, and Jessie's eyes widened and looked away. Amelia broke the silence. "Okayy, I'll leave you both to get to know each other. Jessie, you can leave any time after 7 pm. Mr. Irving, will you be coming to the office today?"

Seth shook his head, getting his hair more tousled. "No, I don't think so. Yesterday was a long day. I need today to rest properly."

Amelia brought out her phone and typed on it. "That's no problem. I'll represent you at the meeting and cancel your other appointments. Jessie, do good. Mr. Irving, goodbye."

He nodded and grunted as he ate the last bite of his ham sandwich. Soon it was just them. Jessie shuffled on her feet, unsure of what to do.

As if reading her mind, Seth spoke. "You can start by cleaning this up." He waved at the counter littered with crumbs and the empty potato chips bag. He pushed the stool back and stood up. As he walked by Jessie, he trembled and grabbed her arm for support.

"Woah!" Jessie tried to hold him up. He turned to look at her with coldness in his eyes and pushed her arm away.

"I don't need your help. Just do your job." With that, he moved out of the room.

"What an asshat!!" She huffed to the empty room. She sighed and walked to the cupboards. Jessie opened them one by one till she came across one with cleaning supplies. She brought out the surface cleanser and a piece of cloth and dropped them on the table. After dumping the wrappers and swept the crumbs into the dumpster, Jessie wiped the surface clean.

"Where do I start from?" She murmured to herself. She straightened the map and decided to begin with the main living room. Jessie looked into the pantry's storage and was relieved to see a mop, vacuum cleaner, and other things she needed. She walked into the large living room and looked around. It was slightly dusty but not too dirty.

She turned on the vacuum cleaner and started cleaning up the place. By the time she was done with the entire living space, plus the dining table, an hour had already passed.

Jessie grabbed a duster and began to brush off the dust from paintings and artifacts. She looked around and found it strange that there was no single picture of himself or his family. There were exciting paintings that depicted art and talent, but none of them looked personal.

"He's not only rude but also strange. Awesome." She muttered as she dusted the paintings. The next stop was the hallway, and surprisingly, it was clean enough, so she just did a quick cleaning. Jessie slowly opened the door of the first bedroom door on the second floor, and it revealed a room that seemed out of place in the entire building.

Every surface was covered, and the dust in the room made Jessie cough. The air in the room was sour, and Jessie had a feeling the windows hadn't been opened in a long time.

She slowly walked to the window and was about to crank it open when she felt a hand grab her shoulder.

"Ahhhhh!" Jessie shrieked and blindly waved her duster in the air. The person pulled her duster from her hand, and when Jessie opened her eyes, she saw it was Seth. His eyes were stormy, and Jessie felt shivers through her body.

"You scared me. I was just-"

"Don't ever touch anything in this room." Seth's hold on her hand was getting painfully tight, and Jessie grimaced at the pain.

"I just wanted to clean-"

"I said, don't come in here ever again." His voice was eerily quiet, but Jessie saw his eyes blazing with anger.

"I'm sorry, I didn't mean to-"

"*IS THAT UNDERSTOOD?!*" Seth roared at her, and Jessie couldn't take it anymore. She burst into tears, pulled her hand away from his hold, and ran from the room. She got to a corner and tried to stop her tears.

"What a horrible man!" She sniffled and wiped her tears. This only strengthened her resolution to earn as much as she could and to get out of there. She didn't care whatever reason he hand behind a large amount of money attached to her cleaning, and she was going to get enough of it.

With her newfound determination, Jessie set to work and cleaned as many rooms as she could. At a point, her movement became so robotic because she was tired and wouldn't stop. When the grandfather clock chimed at 7 pm, Jessie fell into a high stool in the kitchen and downed an entire bottle of water. Her lip gloss was long gone, and she made a mental note to wear more comfortable clothes the next day.

She slowly grabbed her purse and walked out of the kitchen. Jessie looked up the staircase that led to the rooms. He hadn't come down ever since he had yelled at her.

She childishly stuck her tongue into the air. "I hope it stays that way." They pushed the button, and the door slid open, and Jessica was surprised to see it was almost dark. Her phone chimed, and Jessie brought it out to see what the notification was for. A smile graced her lips when she saw her bank account had been credited with her pay for the day.

Jessie did a little skip as she waved down a taxi. I miss mom; I should see her today, she considered. Plus, she could stop running away from Doctor Lucas.

"Hey, I'm going to Laurent Oliver's hospital." She leaned over and said to the taxi driver. Jessie couldn't help but think of the numbers in her bank. She kept checking the message to confirm that it was, in fact, real.

The taxi stopped in front of the hospital, and Jessie walked in. Mandy wasn't on duty, so Jessie didn't have to chat with the unfamiliar nurse. Plus, she wasn't in the mood. Jessie made a stop at Doctor Lucas' office.

"Come in." his voice followed after she knocked on the door. Jessie pushed the door open to reveal the man was reading a book.

"Ah, Miss Lewis. It has been a while." He said pointedly, staring at her over his glasses.

Jessie sat down. "It has. I want to pay for my mom's daily drugs. I'll be starting with that, at least. By the end of the following week, I should have paid a substantial amount."

The look of surprise on Doctor Lucas' face almost made her smirk. In your face! He was just doing his job, and she knew that. But she allowed herself to feel a little bit of self-accomplishment.

Finally, he cleared his throat. "Well, that's um, that's good. Just at the right time because her airway has gotten more inflamed, and the corticosteroids should be able to reduce that."

Jessie sat up and looked at him with worry. "Oh my, is she okay?"

He nodded and spread his hands. "She's alright, but we have to monitor her closely." Jessie's head raced with different scenarios. What if he was just downplaying it? She remembered her mother smoking a lot when Jessie was much younger, and one memory that leads firmly implanted in her head when she asked Hannah, "The pack says smokers are liable to die young. Why do you still do it, mama?"

And she responded, "Oh child, I never said I wanted to live long." Jessie hadn't known what to say, and she still didn't know how to respond to that. She pushed the memory out of her mind and stood up.

Doctor Lucas stood with her and shook her hand. "You can make payment at the front desk."

Jessie nodded and backed out of the room. "Thank you."

She got to the front desk and was surprised to see Mandy. She hadn't seen her in a while.

Mandy beamed at her, her rosy cheeks almost touching her eyes. "Hey you, it has been a while. You don't even come around anymore."

Jessie plopped her elbows on the counter and sighed. "I am so sorry; work has just been crazy."

Mandy's eyebrows rose into her salt and pepper hairline. "Oh? You got a job?"

Jessie nodded. "Yes, all thanks to Mina." She cringed when she realized she hadn't thought to express her gratitude to Mina. She made an emotional note to show gratitude the woman as soon as she saw her.

She asked Mandy, "Is Mina on duty?"

"No. She won't be in till 2 am today."

"Aw, alright. Well, I need to see mom."

Something flickered in Mandy's eyes, and Jessie was scared of what came to her mind first. She shook her head, and it was gone as she had never seen it. She must have imagined it.

"Alright, love. Send my greetings."

"By the way, I want to pay for the drugs."

Mandy wore her glasses and peered at the monitor screen in front of her. "Oh yes, Doctor Lucas just sent the information to me. Would you be making a transfer or be paying in cash?"

The transaction was done quickly enough, and soon, Jessie was on her way into the hallway leading to her mother's room. She hoped she wouldn't be mad that she hadn't seen her in a while.

When Jessie was working at Jerry's, she only visited her mom a couple of times in a week, and soon she got used to that. She didn't know why she was feeling so guilty.

She quickly sent a thank you text to Mina. Hey, you aren't on duty today. Thank you so much. I got the job! I'm so sorry it took me this long to update you.

She slowly pushed the door open, and Jessie saw a nurse carefully adjusted the IV attached to Hannah's wrist. She smiled when she saw Jessie, and although Jessie wasn't sure she knew her, the nurse seemed to recognize Jessie.

She walked up to Jessie and spoke softly. "She's asleep. Please try to be quiet."

Jessie nodded and glanced at the sleeping figure of her mother. The nurse checked the heart monitor once more and left the room.

Jessie softly walked up to the chair beside the bed and sat on it. She looked at her mother's chest go up and down as she inhaled the oxygen through the mask attached to her face.

Her phone chimed, and when Jessie looked at it, she saw it was an email from Mina. *I understand it's okay. That's great! I'm so happy for you. Take care.............*

Even though she wanted to pretend not to see it, Jessie saw how pale and rubbery her mother's skin had become, and the bags under her eyes were dark and heavy.

Tears pooled in her eyes. "Oh, mama. I miss you so much."

Hannah stirred in the bed and slowly opened her eyes. With effort, she turned to look at Jessie. She smiled at her and seemed to mouth her name. With struggle, Hannah tried to sit up.

"Mom, no, no. There's no need. Please lay back." Jessie stared at her mother in exasperation when she saw that she had sat up already. At least she wasn't as weak as Jessie had assumed.

Hannah wasn't done because the next thing she did was rip off the oxygen mask. Jessie stared at her in horror. "Mom! Please, you need to put that back on before the nurse comes in here."

Hannah rolled her eyes. "Glad that the dratted thing is off my face. I can breathe fine–" A heavy cough interrupted her, and she bent double, her sides quivering with the hacking.

Jessie stood up and patted her back. She could feel the panic in her stomach stirring like hornets threatened to be freed. But she pushed it down. She didn't want to scare her mom.

Finally, Hannah stopped coughing and leaned her head against the pillow. "I missed you, and it's been a while."

Jessie felt tears fall down her face, but she quickly wiped them when Hannah frowned at the tears. She had never liked her crying, especially not around her. Hannah always said tears were a sign of weakness. "I miss you too." She decided to stop hiding things from her. "Mama, I lost my job."

Hannah cocked her eyebrows at her. "Well, you were too good for that anyway. And I knew."

"Wait, what?"

Hannah shrugged and closed her eyes. "News reached me that they closed Jerry's. I kind of figured. I was just waiting for you to tell me."

Jessie shook her head and smiled. Even though she was on a hospital bed, she was still one step ahead, like always.

Jessie linked her fingers through her mother's. "I found another one, though. A perfect one."

"I'm glad you did. I am proud of you." Hannah gave her a genuine smile, and her blue eyes sparkled with happiness. Jessie climbed into the tiny space beside her and felt like she was nine years old again.

"Remember the time you went to school with my high heels, and I came to your class and tried to force you to remove it, but you wouldn't listen? Even though the other kids laughed at you, you never cared."

Jessie giggled as she remembered the story. Her strawberry patterned socks peeking out of the open-toe shoes. Her eyes fluttered close when her mother spoke again.

"Remember...when..." The voice seemed to be coming far away as Jessie slipped into a restless sleep.

Chapter 6

A week and three days had passed since Jessie started working at the Irving mansion, and she could count the number of times she had seen Seth.

Amelia had come around a few times, and when Jessie asked why she didn't check her more often, she said, "Oh, there are cameras everywhere, in the house. Mr. Irving can see everything you do." Jessie wasn't sure how to feel about that.

It was a Tuesday afternoon, and surprisingly, she didn't have much to do. She had cleaned many unused rooms the week before, and she was almost done already.

To avoid confrontations with Mr. Irving, she made sure she packed her lunch for the day. But this time, she had forgotten.

Jessie tried to ignore the rumbling of the stomach and vigorously wiped the oven. Soon, she couldn't take it anymore, so she opened the fridge to see what she could quickly eat.

There were piles and piles of Tupperware that the cooking company had dropped for him, and Jessie wondered how much he ate precisely. She saw a bowl of leftover Chinese and took that out.

"Hopefully, he won't want to eat this anymore." She popped it into the microwave and picked out an apple to eat after eating the meal.

Jessie tiptoed to the living room and looked up the stairs. He was still in his bedroom. Good.

The microwave beeped, and she grabbed a mitten to set it on the table.

Jessie was sure she would have choked on the food with the way she rushed it. But she didn't want Seth to see her eating his food. Every time he had called her, it was always something to yell about. Why did she move the figurine on his desk two inches to the left? He liked his duvet folded over twice. Can she stop wearing her shoes into his room? It was exhausting!

She had long abandoned formal clothes for sweats and trainers. Cleaning an entire mansion required a lot of comforts. The only thing comforting her was that she had paid half of the medical bills and her rent. That took a bit of the burden off her shoulders.

The previous day, she had gone to see her mother, she was getting better, and her skin looked much better than she was glad of.

Maybe because she was deep in thought or because she was not concentrating, but Jessie felt a sharp pain as the knife sliced into the skin of her finger while trying to cut the apple.

"Ouch!" She dropped the knife and held her finger that was dripping with blood. Jessie grabbed the paper towel on the counter and tore it a bit to stop the bleeding. But the cut was pretty deep, and soon, the paper towel was wet with blood.

A low growl made Jessie realize she wasn't alone in the room. Head snapped up at the sudden company, and she found Seth standing in the doorway. He stared at her bloodied hand with dark eyes, and it sent a shiver up her spine.

"Oh I-I'm sorry, I cut myself and-"

"Clean that up, now." His voice was raspy, and Jessie took a step back.

"I'm about to-"

"Clean that up!" He roared at her.

Jessie was stunned to silence, and she stared at the angry man in a plain T-shirt and dark joggers. A vein was quivering in his neck, and Jessie noticed how tiny she was compared to him.

So she walked up to him and slapped him. The ferocious on Seth's face was replaced by pure, undiluted shock.

"Don't you dare yell at me ever again! Who do you think you are?! You may have all the money in this world but never yell at me again! I work so hard, and all you have done is treat me like a piece of garbage. I deserve respect." Jessie was crying when she was done, but it wasn't because she was sad; she was so angry that her nails dug into the skin of her palms as she folded them.

Seth stood there and blinked at her, his mouth slightly open. He lifted his hand, and Jessie flinched, but he only raised them to touch the spot she had smacked. Silently, he walked out of the room.

The adrenaline drained out of Jessie, and she shakingly sat at the table. Her finger was still bleeding, and she could feel it throb too.

"Crap, I hope this doesn't get infected." She grabbed another paper towel and dried the blood. Since she definitely would be getting fired, she might as well not touch anything else that belonged to Seth Irving.

Jessie turned to see Seth standing beside the counter with a first aid box. She rubbed her eyes to make sure the loss of blood wasn't making her hallucinate.

He moved close to her and grabbed her finger. His jaws flexed with effort, and he concentrated on her finger. He brought out a bottle of mentholated spirit and cotton balls.

"Hold still." He said to her, but Jessie wasn't moving anyway. She still couldn't believe or understand what was going on.

He gently swabbed at the cut, and Jessie hissed at the stinging pain. Thankfully, the cut stopped bleeding, and Seth wrapped a Band-Aid around her finger. All of that was done within seconds, and Jessie stared at him with flaming cheeks. Had she not smacked the man in the face, yet here he was, cleaning her cut.

"I-er, thank you. I'm grateful. And I'm sorry for..." The rest of the words were unsaid, but Jessie saw him slightly nod, and she sagged with relief. Great, she wouldn't be getting fired then.

Seth grabbed the Mini first aid kid, and Jessie cursed inwardly when she caught herself admiring how his muscles flexed under the tight shirt he was wearing.

When he got to the hallway, he turned to look at her. "Just don't...cut yourself again. I'm serious."

Okayyyy. "It's not like I will go around slicing my fingers, haha." Jessie soon shut her mouth when she realized she was the only one laughing.

Seth just stared at her for some minutes before walking out of the room. Well, damn. Jessie disposed of the bloodied tissue and looked at her wrapped-up finger. There was nothing she could execute with her left hand because the cut's pain put a strain on her entire hand. She looked at the clock and sighed aloud. She still had two hours left till she could go home.

Jessie walked into the living room and sat gingerly on the leather couch. The chair was so soft that she sank into it. "Aaah... this feels good." She closed her eyes for some seconds, only for them to fly open when she heard footsteps come down the stairway. Jessie struggled to come out of the couch, but Seth came downstairs just in time to catch her wrestling with his couch.

Jessie thought she saw something like amusement in his eyes, but it was gone. She froze when she looked at him in a dark blue suit. She had always thought he was good-looking in his sweats and with a stubble covering his jawline. But he had shaved, and his hair was still glistening with droplets of water. Like everything else, his suit's cut looked mainly made for him as it showed off his attractive physique.

His Louis Vuitton dress shoes softly tapped the tiles as he walked up to her. "I have a very essential meeting that I can't keep pushing, and I won't be back till later today. I hope you won't be leaving the house till you are done because I set the doors to lock as soon as you step outside automatically."

Jessie finally stood up from the couch and tried not to stare at him too much. "Oh, of course, I will be here till my shift is over."

Seth nodded and walked out of the house. Jessie peeked out of the window and watched him drive a dark Ferrari out of the automatic gate and into the road.

"Whew! I wonder how many more cars he has." Jessie said as she turned to look around the house in excitement. She had always wanted to look through the house as some sort of treasure hunt. And what better place to start with than the forbidden room that Seth told her to stay away from.

"I'll get into so much trouble if he finds out?" But did that stop her? Nope.

Jessie climbed up the stairs and into the long hallway that looked creepy now that she was all by herself. The figures on the wallpaper seemed to be staring at Jessie as she passed. A shiver went up to her spine, and she shuddered. "All of a sudden, I don't like this house much anymore."

Finally, she stared at the door leading to the room that Seth had told her not to enter. She turned the door and saw that it was locked. "Of course, it's locked."

She huffed and stared at it as the door could open under her intense stare. That didn't work, so she did the next dumbest thing. She walked to Seth's room.

Luckily, the door wasn't locked, so it slid open. Seth's room was always dark, and it didn't matter if you drew the curtains apart. The windowpanes themselves were a dark shade, and so was the interior of his room.

The walls were the darkest shade of grey, and a candle chandelier hung from the ceiling but was turned off. A large painting of a hill was placed above his bed, and the predominant colors were grey and black. A gold-colored quilt was hastily spread across the bed, and Jessie absentmindedly straightened it.

As much as she wanted to look around the vast space, Jessie decided to get straight to business. The first place to look was the table of drawers beside his bed. She opened the first drawer but only found some receipts and a ring. The next drawer had a sleeping mask and some painkillers. There was also a thread used for stitching wounds. Jessie wondered what it might be for. The last drawer was empty.

Disappointed, Jessie stood up and looked around. She had no idea where it could be. Where would he keep a tiny key? An idea popped into her mind, and Jessie rushed to the dressing table. There was a small jewelry box, and when Jessie opened it, she smiled. Right in the middle of the rings and bracelets, the key sat among the gold jewelry.

"Gotcha!" Jessie grabbed it and quietly shut the room door. She walked back to the forbidden door and inserted the key into the lock. Her heart hammered when the lock clicked open, and Jessie slowly pushed the door to reveal the dusty room.

It was the same as she had left it before; dusty. The flowery curtains that hung from the rods were faded and dirty. As expected, everything was still covered up, and Jessie coughed when she inhaled a little bit of dust.

The room looked like it would be cozy without all dirt and dust that covered it. Jessie could imagine the curtains, without dust, would be bright yellow. She pulled off the piece of cloth covering furniture and revealed a mahogany table. It was smooth, and although it looked like it had been there for a while, it was relatively new.

Jessie sat on the bed and coughed again when dust flew from the mattress. "Why won't he just let me clean this room? It's so dusty in here."

She rested on the bed and looked around. There was nothing much to see, and that wasn't very pleasant. Jessie was getting onto her feet when her heel kicked something under the bed. It was a medium-sized brown box with tiny drawings on it. It was a little bit heavy, but Jessie was able to haul it onto the bed.

Luckily, it wasn't locked, so she just opened the lid of the box. Picture frames and papers were turned upside down, with their bottoms facing up. Jessie picked up the first item in the box; it was a picture frame. Jessie turned it over, and she looked at the image, confused. It was a picture of a younger Seth in a garden, and a beautiful small woman was in his arms. The picture was a little bit old and unclear, but Jessie could see that she had red hair. Seth looked so happy in the picture that she couldn't believe he was the same sullen man.

There were more pictures of them together. There was one where she held the camera to capture them in some pottery room. It seemed like the lady was a photographer as there were pictures of the backyard, the view, the hallways, and even Seth.

The pictures changed, and soon, the red-haired woman always had a hand on her stomach in every picture. Soon, Jessie could see a clear bump, and there was no doubt that she was pregnant. The pictures stopped abruptly, and there were only papers. One certain piece of paper caught her eye because there was a wax seal at the bottom. It was typed in beautiful calligraphy.

Jessie read out loud, "Seth Irving born in Italy & Adell born in Sweden. Married on May 9, 2010." Was Seth married? Jessie brought out her phone and typed in both their names to see what popped up. She gasped when she read the headlines. Wife to Billionaire Seth Irving found mauled by unknown wild animals. Annabelle Irving discovered in the forest behind the Irving Mansion.

Jessie gasped and put a hand to her mouth. Thankfully, there were no pictures of Annabelle from the incident. Was she dead? "Oh my god, that's horrible." She felt an overwhelming pity for Seth and couldn't imagine what it must have felt like.

A howl pierced the air, and Jessie jerked up from the floor, where she had been sitting. She rushed over to the window to look outside. Just by the gate was an enormous dog. It howled again and scratched at the gate.

"What the heck?" Jessie quickly shut the box and put it back in its position. She looked around to make sure nothing was out of place and threw the cloth back onto the desk. She locked the room and raced to Seth's room. Jessie carefully placed the key in the middle of the jewelry and quickly rushed downstairs.

"Oh shoot." She remembered what Seth had said about the door locking automatically if she leaves the house. Jessie removed her left trainer and opened the door. She quickly wedged the shoe under the door and hobbled outside. She didn't want to go outside the gate if the dog attacked her, but she stared at it through the iron bars then ran through the middle of the gate.

The dog looked unusual for a dog, and Jessie couldn't recognize the breed. It was scratching at the gate, and saliva hung from its yellow teeth. Jessie was a lover of dogs, but for the first time, she was terrified. It focused its yellow eyes on Jessie and went silent. Despite how feral it looked, his eyes showed intelligence as he studied her. He cocked his ears and looked into the forest like it had heard something from there.

He snarled at Jessie and ran into the forest. The whole ordeal spooked Jessie, but she was glad it has come. "Hopefully, it doesn't come back." She peeped out to make sure it was gone, and indeed, it was.

Jessie walked back into the house with a sigh of relief, dislodged her shoe, and shut the door. It was seconds later before she realized what she had just done.

"Noooo!" She yanked at the door, and a robotic voice said, "Automatic lock initiated."

Jessie ran to the kitchen. A door led to the pool behind the house; maybe she could find a way out. She pulled at the door, and nothing. Just the same robotic voice was saying, "Automatic lock initiated." She raced throughout the house, trying all the exit doors, but it was all the same.

Finally, she sat on the couch, exhausted. She checked the time; it was a few minutes after 7 pm. "Lord, when will he be back?"

Drained of all her energy, Jessie decided to heat a bowl of chicken soup that the cooking company had brought. She poured herself a glass of orange juice and sat in front of the wide TV screen.

Jessie stared at her cellphone with no missed calls or texts. She hadn't bothered to set plans with anyone, no dates, nothing. She decided to set weekend plans with Lucy. Jessie decided that she wanted more friends and tried to get closer to other people. But growing up as the daughter of the lady who did odd jobs, smoked, and gave the middle finger to anyone who questioned her parenting, Jessie didn't grow up with enough of her peers to develop social skills.

And love? There had been a few dates, but the last time she had a boyfriend was 24, and he decided they weren't compatible.

He ended up cheating on her with his 'best friend.' Since then, she decided to focus on her work and abandon love. Not that she had had the time anyway. But sometimes, it got lonely. Especially now that her Sundays were free for the first time in a while. She wished she could curl up with a cup of cocoa and discuss with someone about random things and laugh while the stars illuminated the sky.

It got dark quickly, and she tried to call Amelia; maybe she could give her Seth's phone number. "Hi, this is Amelia Knowles"

"Oh, thank God Amelia I-"

"- *I'm not on the phone right now. Please leave a message after the beep.*"

Jessie sighed and hung up. There was no need anymore. She dropped her cellphone on the table and leaned back on the chair. A few minutes later, her eyes started to shut as sleep took over. Soon, she couldn't fight it, and Jessie dreamt of snarls and yellow eyes.

Jessie woke up to the sound of a door being shut. The lights in the living room had dimmed automatically, so the room was quite dark. A figure stood by the door and turned up the light; it was Seth.

"Jessie? What are you doing here?" He had removed his tie, and his suit jacket hung from his arm. He looked tired yet alert.

Jessie rubbed her eyes and sat up. She rubbed her arms as the weather had gotten colder. "Oh, I'm sorry. It's a long story, and I just got shut in here."

Jessie saw something like amusement flicker in his eyes, but it was gone and replaced with concern. "Isn't it a bit cold in here? You could have turned up the heat."

"Ah well, we don't all live in top techy houses. I'm not sure I know how to do that." This time Seth smiled at Jessie's words and walked up to a panel on the Far East wall. He punched in some numbers, and Jessie felt the room get noticeably warmer. How come she never noticed that?

"Thank you." Seth nodded and sat on the sofa opposite her. He cleared his throat and turned to look at her. "Have you eaten?"

Jessie turned around to make sure she was the one he was talking to. "Er, yes, I have. There was chicken soup. I-I hope it's okay that I ate that?"

He shrugged and shut his eyes. "It doesn't matter. I can't eat it all anyway."

"What about you?"

"I already ate."

Jessie nodded and leaned back on the couch. The silence between them stretched, but it was comfortable.

"Why are you suddenly nice to me?" wait, had she blurted that out? Oh crap, she did.

Seth looked at her incredulously. "You don't want me to?"

"No, no, it's not that. Ever since I started this job, you have been cold to me, and I slapped you once, and all of a sudden, you are asking me if I've eaten your food."

"I suppose it was a resetting sound." Jessie stared at him. Did Seth Irving have a sense of humor, or was she hallucinating?

He sat up and continued. "I believe I'm your boss, and telling you the right thing to do shouldn't come off as mean."

Jessie refrained the urge to roll her eyes. Aha, there was the Seth Irving she knew.

"But I admit I was in the wrong about yelling at you for cutting your finger. That, I apologize for. "

Jessie reluctantly accepted his apology. She nodded in response and shut her eyes. Seth spoke again. "How did you end up locked in here again?"

"Ah, that. There was this huge black dog scratching at the gate and howling. I ended up coming down and —woah! Are you okay? You look pale."

Seth was digging his nails into the chair, and his skin looked pale and ashen. His eyes were wide, and he stared into nothing. "W-what did it look like?"

"It was huge. Huge for a dog. Reminded me of an enormous, black Bobo. And it had yellow eyes. Seems like signs of Jaundice, poor--"

Seth flew from the chair and grabbed her by the arm. "He didn't see you, did he? Answer me!"

He? "Ow! You're hurting me. Of course, it saw me. I went outside to chase it away."

Seth stared at her with horror, and Jessie's palms went cold. He was scaring her. Finally, he said, í don't know if that is foolish or brave. Maybe both. Listen, you have to stay here. Your life is in danger."

Jessie yanked her arms from his hold. "It's just a dog. Why are you scaring me? Are you doing this on purpose?" Her eyes welled up as she considered the fact that he could be doing this to scare her. "There's no way I'm coming to live here. Is this a way of trying to make me work beyond my usual hours?"

Seth slapped his forehead and paced around the room. "This can't happen again. It can't!"

Jessie sat down on the couch and stared at him. Beads of sweat had gathered on his forehead and neck. Jessie decided she was tired, so she walked up to him and smacked him.

He looked at her with shock. "You can't keep doing this."

"I'm sorry, but you needed it." It did work because he had calmed down and seemed to realize where he was. Jessie grabbed his large hand and led him to the couch. "It was just a big dog."

Seth opened his mouth to argue, but he decided against it and shook his head. He stood up and turned to leave the living room. I'm going to bed. You can sleep in any of the available rooms if you want to."

Jessie nodded. "Thank you." She followed him up the staircase and into the hallway leading to his room. She decided to take the room right beside his, and Jessie convinces herself that it wasn't because she was scared or anything.

As she opened the door leading to her room, Seth spoke. "I'm sorry, Jessie." Before she could ask him what it was, he was sorry for, and he had entered his room and locked the door behind him. She shuddered and opened the door to the room beside his. She switched on the light to reveal a blue with mainly dark blue hues. Luckily for her, she had only cleaned the room a few days ago, so everything was fresh and clean.

Jessie sighed when she remembered she would be sleeping in the clothes she had been wearing all day. She decided to open the closet, and by chance, there was an oversized hoodie hanging in it. She quickly stripped and entered the bathroom. Jessie seemed when she saw that there was a Jacuzzi in the bathroom. She had never been in one but was able to work it all out from the shows she had watched.

"Who knew those late-night TV shoes would help?" Jessie asked as she allowed the warm jets of water to soothe her body. She didn't spend too much in the water, even though she wanted to, because she was already feeling chilly.

Jessie pulled on the oversized hoodie and jumped into bed. She purposely pushed out all the day's discoveries the weird experiences and decided to sleep. She closed her eyes and counted sheep in her head, and before she knew it, Jessie was fast asleep. Jessie woke up to the sound of someone breathing beside her. She sat up with a startle but soon calmed down when she saw it was Seth.

Why was he here? She watched as his eyes moved under his eyelids and his fists remained clenched. Jessie slowly reached out and unclenched his tight fist. Seth's eyes sprung open and he turned to look at her.

"Hey." His voice was raspy but clear. "Sorry I came here. I- I just... I didn't feel like being alone." Jessie's heart melted a bit and she laid down to look at him.

She whispered, "It's okay." The silence stretched between them as she looked into Seth's eyes. Jessie held her breath as Seth lifted a hand and stroke her hair. Something in her belly stirred as she closed her eyes to enjoy the moment. She felt warm breath on her lips and when she opened her eyes, she was staring into Seth's eyes.

"Can I kiss you?"

Jessie swallowed and nodded. The moist warmth of Seth's lips overwhelmed her and something that started as short and sweet grew into a moment that was heated and fiery. Seth slowly undressed Jessie and looked at her, seeking for consent. She nodded and tugged at his shirt.

She wasn't wearing anything under and gasped when she felt the touch of his fingers in her.

"You are so wet wow." Seth muttered into her neck and he unbuckled his pants.

Jessie mounted him and began to slowly move her hips. Seth kissed her lips and explored the wonders of her mouth with his tongue. She touched his chest and he bit lightly on a lip, a sharp tinge quickly filled her mouth. Seth wrapped his fingers with hers and gripped them as he looked at her with wonder.

As she moved faster, Seth bounced with her rhythm and together, they erupted. They both laid on the bed, eyes wide open with the memory of their lovemaking swimming in Jessie's head.

"That was..."

Seth finished for her. "Mind blowing."

Chapter 7

The sun had risen by the time Jessie by the time Jessie opened her eyes the next morning. At first, Jessie had looked around the room in alarm, wondering where she was. But the memories of the previous day came rushing to her, and she sank into the bed.

There was a loud bang on the door, and Jessie realized all she had on was an oversized hoodie she had found. She quickly wrapped the comforter around her waist and hobbled towards the door. She opened the door to reveal a freshly showered Seth.

Jessie couldn't look into his eyes and she hoped he wouldn't bring up their sexcapade the previous night. Thankfully, he didn't. Droplets of water glistened in his hair, and he smelt faintly of peppermint and a woody scent. It was an odd yet pleasant smell. He had jeans on and had donned a grey polo shirt. Jessie had noticed that most of his clothes were dark-colored.

He cleared his throat. "Good morning. I see you found my college sweater useful."

"Oh my, I'm so sorry. Are you still using it?"

He shook his head. "So, I'm assuming you didn't bring any extra clothes."

"No. it's not liked I planned to get stuck in here."

"Wait here." He walked away from the room and entered his. Jessie stood in the door frame, comforter wrapped around her waist, and she felt silly. Seth came back and had a bundle of clothes in his hands and threw them at Jessie.

So, she had been holding the bulging comforter with one hand, but due to reflex, she stretched forth her hands to catch the clothes, and the comforter around her waist came tumbling down.

Jessie's face burnt bright red. The hoodie wasn't so short; it touched reached mid-thighs, but she still felt extremely uncomfortable. Thankfully, Seth simply ignored the whole thing and walked out of the room. Jessie shut the door and put a hand to her hammering heart.

"Well, that was awkward." She checked the bathroom for a toothbrush, and fortunately for her, there was a brand new toothbrush in the cabinet. She took out the toothpaste and brushed her teeth. Jessie stared in the mirror and touched the split ends in her hair. When the weekend rolled by, she would get a better haircut.

Her hair had gotten a bit longer, and she still wasn't sure if she liked it or not. One person that Jessie had been continuously thinking of was Aimee. They had texted few times in the last month, but Jessie decided she would travel out of the state to see her. It could double as a vacation for herself and her mom. Hopefully, by then, she would be better.

She had spoken to Doctor Lucas not too long ago, and he said Hannah was getting much better. She was still far from being back to her usual self, but Jessie had high hopes. She rinsed the toothbrush when she was done and decided she would take it home. She opened the cabinet and saw a pack of rose-scented bath bombs.

"Oooh, this will smell so good." Jessie was excited to enter the Jacuzzi again. She had had a lovely bathing experience with it and wanted to do it all over again. She threw the bath bomb into the water and watched it fizzle and dissolve into the bath.

Jessie climbed in and sighed with relief as the water soothed her body. Since she had to get to work, Jessie couldn't spend all morning in the bath, so she stepped out of it and grabbed a towel. She dried her hair and admired how it fell into waves even though it wasn't scorched. She'd leave it that way.

The bundles of clothes that Seth had handed to her were matching track pants and a tracksuit. Although it was still a little bit big for her, it was one of his old clothes that didn't size him anymore. Jessie couldn't help but notice that the outfits smelled like him.

She put on the clothes and rolled the ends of the tracks so they didn't get in the way. She pulled out the hair tie off her wrist and gathered her hair to pack it up.

No, I want to let it down today, she thought. Jessie reluctantly dropped her hand and allowed her hair to flow freely.

Jessie laid the bed and bunched up the towel so she could wash it. She wanted everything to be just the way she had met it.

She was walking down the corridor when she overheard Seth talking loudly at someone over the phone. The study he was in wasn't too far from her room, which was why she could hear him.

"Why are you just telling me about it now? Mr. Ferguson will be there? Damn. Since when did they mention the interview, and did you notify me? Did you? I can't believe this. I have to be there."

Jessie decided she had heard enough and quietly walked down the staircase. Whatever it was, he sounded agitated by it, and she made a mental note to stay out of his way.

She decided she would clean the laundry room today. Although Seth did his laundry himself, Jessie decided to do that herself today as a way of saying thank you. The laundry room was one of the smallest rooms in the house, but it was still bigger than her bedroom at her apartment. There were two washing machines placed side by side, and a basket of clothes was placed beside them.

The room was airy and spacy, and unlike the dark hues and colors of the house, the wallpaper was teal and white. Something told Jessie that Annabelle designed the room herself. Floral curtains fluttered slowly as the breeze from the open window softly pushed it around.

Jessie grabbed the basket and tried to sort it by color, and put the darker clothes in the wash first. She dug into the laundry basket and felt something wet.

"Huh, what is that?" She pulled at the material only to reveal a bloodied inner shirt that had three long slashes in the middle.

"What the heck?" Jessie held out the messed-up piece of cloth and stared at it in shock. It was so bloody that it had even stained other clothes at the bottom of the basket. Jessie inspected the slashes, and they were ripped from end to end. It looked like it had been cut through by something sharp. Maybe a knife or...a claw?

Was this Seth's, and if he had wounds from the slashes, how the heck had he not ended in a hospital. Jessie was afraid that she might get answers she didn't want to hear if she asked questions. Suddenly, the house didn't seem as friendly and as beautiful as she had initially thought. It felt like a cage.

Jessie decided to set the cloth aside and wash the other ones. When she was done putting the other clothes through the wash, Jessie put the bloodied shirt into the washing machine. She looked into the transparent hood and watched the soapy water turn red. What was going on? Did she want to know?

By the time she was done washing the clothes, the sun was shining brightly, and the sky was bright blue. She opened the door leading to the backyard and held the laundry basket filled with wet clothes. There were lines, and Jessie pegged the clothes to the line to dry by the sun.

Maybe Seth had another way he dried his clothes, but this was the only way she knew, and it was effective. Jessie was pegging the last pants when she heard the gate's automated sound whenever someone opened it. Who could it be?

She walked into the laundry room and shut the backyard door close. She dropped the now-empty laundry basket and left the room. Jessie walked into the living room only to see Amelia and Seth whispering ferociously to each other. They quieted when they saw Jessie walk into the room.

Was she getting fired? Oh no, she couldn't afford that now. She still had to pay for her mother's healthcare and-

"Jessie darling, it has been a while. How are you faring? You have been doing a great job, too. Look at the place!" For the first time since Jessie had gotten to know Amelia, she was dressed in casual slacks and a lacy blouse with red strappy sandal heels.

Her long blond hair flowed down to her waist, and although she looked put together, the strain in her eyes betrayed her.

Jessie was surprised when Amelia hugged her, but she awkwardly hugged her back. "Er, I'm fine. Thank you."

Amelia led her to the sofa, and Jessie turned to look at Seth, who was sitting opposite them. He avoided her gaze, and a vein on his forehead throbbed. "Listen, Jessie, I need your help. We need your help?"

Jessie stared at her with concern. "Is everything okay?"

"Yes, yes. Actually, not really. We are in a bit of um, a sticky situation?"

"Well, how can I help?"

Amelia glanced at Seth one last time and rubbed her forehead. She sighed and said, "We need you to be Seth's date."

Jessie froze and resisted the urge to burst into manic laughter. Maybe there was a joke she was missing. "What?"

Amelia stood up and squeezed her face like she was going to burst into tears. "Please do this for me, or I'll lose my job. I forgot to set a reminder for the event, and it's this evening, and I don't know what to do. I-I need your help."

Jessie had no idea what to do at this point. She looked at Seth, and he had his head in his hands. Why wasn't he saying anything? "Why can't you go?"

Amelia rolled her eyes. "Everyone at the event knows I'm his assistant. I can't just show up as my boss's date. It won't look okay on the press. Plus, I just got engaged last week."

Her eyes got brighter, and Amelia smiled as she touched the diamond ring on her finger, as if reminding herself that it was still there. Jessie felt a pang of sadness in her heart. She had assumed that Jessie was single, and she wasn't wrong. There was nothing wrong with being single anyway, Jessie convinced herself.

"Why must he go with a date?" This time it was Seth that answered Jessie. "Mr. Ferguson is a bit of a... traditional man. He is organizing this event for couples only. He seems to think men in relationships have a greater sense of responsibility. Bullshit, if you ask me. But I need to sign an essential deal, which is my best shot at winning him over."

Jessie looked him over. There was a look of desperation in his eyes, and she wondered what exactly the deal was and why it was so important to him. She didn't see how it would be of use to her in any way other than making her feel like a fraud among affluent people. Yet, she wanted to help him. She wanted to help Amelia. She wasn't sure why but she couldn't say no.

"Okay, but I don't have any fancy dress to--"

"That's fine. I will get stylists and designers over. All you have to do is sit. Thank you, Jessie, I owe you!" Amelia squealed with excitement and gave Jessie a tight hug. She whipped out her phone and walked out of the living room to make calls.

Soon it was just Seth and Jessie, sitting across from each other. Seth spoke first. "Thank you."

Jessie shrugged. "You're welcome." Then she added an afterthought. "I have a question to ask."

Seth turned to look at her inquisitively. "What is it?"

"Yesterday, you completely freaked out when I told you that weird dog came to the gate. Why?"

Seth laughed, but it wasn't the humorous type. It was a sad laugh because he sobered immediately after. "You shouldn't know some things, Jessie. Curiosity killed the cat."

"And satisfaction brought it back." Jessie was getting agitated now. "You were pale, and you don't want me to know?"

Seth stood up from the couch and started to walk away. "Trust me; you do not want to know."

Jessie watched his receding figure and had to bite her lip to prevent herself from yelling out loud. All of it was so frustrating and tiring. Why couldn't he just offer a simple explanation, and where did she stand in all of this? It felt like none of it should be her business, yet she had a gut feeling she just walked into something dangerous. Jessie didn't have much time to think about it because soon enough, people holding hangers filled with clothes, makeup boxes, hair curlers, and more pooled into the room where she was.

"Well, that was fast." She murmured to herself, feeling uncomfortable under the intense steer of the stylists.

Amelia spread her hands into the air, "Well, get to work! We have limited time. Move it, people!"

Everyone scrambled and rushed to Jessie. They all seemed to speak at the same time. "We will have to do a wax before anything?"

Jessie looked around frantically. She had to get waxed? Those things hurt like crazy. "Um, I don't need a wax. I can just-"

A familiar-looking older man with long hair and a beret pursed his lips at Jessie. He clapped twice, and the entire room went quiet. Jessie was both impressed and frightened at the same time.

"Darling. For Mr. Irving to book me on such short notice mean he expects the best. It's not really about what you want or not; you need to look extraordinaire. I am after all, Alfonso Luca."

Jessie gasped when she heard his name. The Alfonso Luca was the one styling her? He had styled top pop stars, celebrities, and even politicians. He smiled at her reaction. "I hope you will cooperate?"

Starstruck, Jessie could only nod. Alfonso turned to the room and waved his hand into the hair. "Okay, people, let's move."

They ended up having to walk to the recreational room, where a long bench was to be used for her waxing procedure. Two women were in charge, and they smiled at Jessie to reassure her it wouldn't be painful.

She laid flat on the bench and closed her eyes. The first waxing stripped was placed on her right leg, and Jessie howled when they pulled it off. Luckily, there was a cream that neutralized the pain, and though Jessie groaned when they pulled off the strips as they waxed her, she looked forward to the cooling feeling of the neutralizing cream.

Soon, they were done, and Jessie ran her hand all over her body. Her skin felt so smooth, and she loved it. "I should do this more," she said to herself. The pain was so worth it.

Jessie had her eyebrows shaped in the next hour, got her nails done, and had her hair up in curlers. She sat down, and people bustled around her, prodding her and polishing her to look like some sort of celebrity.

When it was time to choose a dress, Alfonso attended to her himself. Someone wheeled in a movable cloth hanger, and there were different dresses of various lengths and colors. Jessie felt like she was playing dress-up, and she was excited to see how it would all turn out. Her hand moved to a minimalist straight white knee-length dress, but Alfonso smacked her hand away.

"Why is that even on the hanger? Take that ridiculous thing away, anybody."

Jessie swallowed when she saw the price tag on one of those dresses. There was no way she could afford that. "I'm sorry, I can't afford this."

"Honey, Mr. Alfonso already paid." Jessie looked at the multiple outfits on the hanger and tried to calculate how much everything must be worth, but she decided not to. It would be embarrassing if he had a panic attack right here.

She tried on a dark brown dress with lace sleeves. Alfonso looked at it for some minutes before shaking his head. "Nah, too conventional. On peut faire mieux. Next!"

Jessie must have tried on five different dresses, and all Alfonso said was, "Bland. Boring. You look like a child's glitter project. This dress should be for a presentation, not a wedding." Finally, the tired assistant picked out a dress from the middle of the hanger, and Alfonso smiled.

He held it out to Jessie. "Try this one." It was a short dress with a flared skirt. The dress's navy blue soft hue as Jessie did a little twirl in front of the mirror. There was a tiny bow at the waist, but that was the only design on it. She couldn't help but admire how classy she looked in it.

She walked out of the bathroom and into the room where Alfonso and his assistants were. He beamed when he saw her and exclaimed, "Spectaculaire! That is how you look. Ouch, I love this so much. Angelo, pass me the pumps in that grey box." A tiny man ran and removed shiny nude pumps from the box and put them on for Jessie.

Alfonso nodded and clapped as he looked at the total ensemble. "Perfecto. I love this. Okay, we need to pick out the dress for dinner. We don't have time!"

It didn't take too much to pick out a dress for the reception because Jessie fell in love immediately she saw it. She pointed at the dress. "I want that." Alfonso smiled at her and nodded. "Good choice."

He removed the dress and handed it to her. Jessie walked into the bathroom and tried on the dress. She gasped when she saw her reflection. It was a form-fitting strapless gold sequined dress. There was a lace covering around the waistline, and it accentuated the slim curve of her body. The back of the dress was open in a V-cut and ended right at the end of her spine.

She walked out of the bathroom in the dress, and everyone gasped as they stared at Jessie. Amelia walked into the room and beamed when she saw Jessie. "Wow, you look amazing." Jessie picked out black heels with tiny jewels on them to go with the dress.

Amelia clapped and waved her hands in the air. "Okay, people, we need to move. We have an hour till the event begins."

In the next hour, Jessie had gotten blond extensions added to her hair to make it longer. A professional makeup artist touched up her face but made sure Jessie still looked natural.

Amelia sat beside Jessie as she was getting the final touches on her makeup. "You will wear the formal dress first, then change into the dinner gown for the reception. We have booked a nearby hotel to InterContinental's, that's the name of the venue by the way, and you will change in the room. The makeup artiste will also retouch your look."

At this moment was when Seth stepped into the room. He had been inside his room since Jessie started getting ready. Only one assistant had been with him since he didn't require much to get ready. Jessie was aware that her eyes had widened, but she couldn't stop looking at him.

His usually messy hair was swept back in perfection. His stubble had been shaved, and his sculpted chin was on full display. He was wearing a grey tux with gold designs on it that glittered under the light. There was a gold wolf head lapel pin on his tux and it matched his gold tie.

Jessie noticed how good he looked and polished the look. He paused to look at Jessie, and something passed in his eyes, and Jessie could have sworn it was surprising. He looked away and walked up to Amelia.

Jessie felt something like disappointment go through her, but she quickly pushed it down. It didn't matter anyway.

Amelia spoke to Jessie, "Okay, you and Mr. Irving will be leaving now. I'll take care of this place. Have a good time and call me if you need me."

Jessie smiled and hugged her. "Thank you." Amelia was taken aback by the sudden display of affection, but she hugged her back and patted her. Jessie smoothed her dress and slowly walked out of the house with Seth right behind her. He walked into the garage and pointed a key at a grey Ferrari. A beep resounded through the garage as the doors unlocked. He walked to the passenger seat and opened the door for her. Jessie resisted the urge to blush and only said," Thank you."

He walked to his side of the car and sat in the driver's seat. Jessie admired the number of buttons on the dashboard and the feel of the car's expensive interior. She turned to Seth. "Wow, this is nice."

For the first time that day, Seth gave a genuine smile. "Yeah, it's one of my favorite cars. One thing I love about it is the interior. The grey leather goes nicely with the grey exterior and-- oh sorry. I'm ranting." He cleared his throat and revved the car out of the driveway and into the road. Jessie turned her head to the window and hid a smile. So this cold billionaire was a car geek, cute. *Wait for what?* She said in her head. *Do I think he is that way?* Jessie turned to look at him and noticed how perfect his side profile was.

"I guess he is." She murmured to herself.

Seth turned to look at her. "What's that?"

Woah. How had he heard her?

"Oh, I-I said you look nice."

Jessie couldn't believe her eyes when she saw a red spot appear on his cheeks. He looked at her and tried to rub his hair before remembering it had been styled. "Oh, er, thanks. You look... really nice too." This time, the redness appeared on Jessie's cheeks as she looked down at her hands. They were quiet for a moment before Jessie spoke again.

"So, what is this meeting or event all about?"

"Ah, that. A bunch of rich people come together and pretend they care about society. I'm here to see Mr. Ferguson."

Jessie blurted out. "But what are you doing about the society?"

Seth glanced at her as he made a turn. He smirked and shook his head. "Have you heard about the Rest Your Head project? It was a community of houses mainly built for homeless people, and it was completely free."

"Yes, I have. What has that got to do with-"

"It's mine. The houses, everything. I'm in charge of it."

Jessie gawped at him. That was a project that cost millions of dollars, yet the benefactor wasn't in the limelight.

She opened and closed her mouth for few seconds before finally speaking. "But why aren't you taking credit for it? It's a huge deal."

"I don't think I need to be known for doing something like this. These people need the houses, and that's all that matters. I'll rather stay anonymous."

Jessie stared at him and felt something flutter in her belly. It was something she hadn't felt in such a long time. It felt like...no, it couldn't be. She shook her head and caught her reflection in the window as it reflected her look.

The extension added to her hair made it easier for them to curl her hair into fat ringlets that bounced as she moved her head. The makeup accentuated the high cheekbones she didn't know she had, and the bold red lipstick made her lips look fuller. She smiled at her reflection, and for once, she decided to pretend that she wasn't a cleaner, pretending to be her boss' date. Instead, she was a dignified woman on a date with a handsome man.

The sun had gone down when the Ferrari pulled up in front of a tall, well-lit building with people in fur and silk pooling in and out. Jessie turned to speak to Seth, and her eyes widened as she saw him leaning towards her. He was moving so close that she could smell his aftershave on his face. Her heart raced as she stared into his eyes. He looked away and unlocked her safety belt.

"We have arrived," he said. Jessie felt her face burn as she realized she had thought something else. Seth got down from the driver seat and walked to her side, and opened the door for her, once again. She got down, and he shut the door and handed the key to the valet that had been waiting.

Jessie stared at the people coming down from expensive cars and donned fur jackets, Chanel bags, and feathered hats, and she felt her heartbeat furiously. They noticed her and Seth and began whispering as they walked into the building.

"W-will this work?" She looked up at Seth nervously.

"Yes, it will. It has to. Just remember you are Morgan Chase, and you are an art teacher in London. If they want to Google you, just tell them that you are extremely private and don't post your life on the internet. Come on, let's do this."

Jessie nodded, and they walked to the entrance of the event center. As Seth led her into the vast hall, Jessie realized one thing with his hand on the small of her back, and she gasped silently when it popped into her head. She had a crush on Seth.

Chapter 8

Massive chandeliers lit up the enormous hall, and Jessie found herself looking up at the high ceiling. As soon as she and Seth walked into the hall, all eyes were on them. The women, both young and old, looked at Jessie with a mixture of curiosity and jealousy.

The men looked at Seth with envy as he walked into the room, an aura of importance oozing from him. Jessie could hear the whispers as they walked past a group of older women who gossiped behind their wine glasses. 'Is this his new lady?' 'How come I didn't hear about it?' 'she must be exceptional. He hasn't been with any lady since Annabelle.'

Jessie saw Seth's fist tighten as he heard his wife's name. She knew he was also listening.

Two women about Jessie's age hurdled together and stared at her with envy. They looked her up and down and squeezed their faces at her. Just to spite them, Jessie linked her hand through Seth's arm. He had a surprised look on his face, but he didn't remove her hand. The room had been arranged with four chairs around each decorated table. There were reservation cards on the tables with names boldly written on them.

On the stage was a middle-aged woman in a matching peach suit set, and she was saying something into a microphone when she noticed them walking in. "Aha, Mr. Irving, CEO of Irving group of companies, just walked in. Welcome, welcome."

Seth gave a brief wave before settling into their reserved seat at the front. He pulled out the chair for Jessie and gave her a light kiss on the cheek. He whispered, "Sorry, I just want us to look more convincing."

Jessie blushed, but she nodded. She looked up to meet the curious gaze of an elderly woman in a navy blue dress. Seth greeted the elderly woman and her husband since they were the second two who shared the table.

The woman on the stage rounded up what she was saying and said something that finally caught Jessie's attention. "Now, I will be inviting to the stage the pioneer of this event, Mr. Ferguson."

Polite applause broke through the room as around, and the short bald man climbed the stage. His belly was bursting through his stomach, but Jessie couldn't help but think of him as a cheerful grandfather. He beamed as he held the microphone and waved at everyone.

"Thank you for coming to the Hercules Fundraising. Let's make the society better."

Another set of polite claps rang through the air. Jessie looked around and saw that while Mr. Ferguson may have good intentions, the bored looks on most people's faces showed that they weren't there to help.

The moment he got off the stage, the event commenced. Seth held out his hand for Jessie to grab, and they moved around the room. There were different sections to raise money. There was an ongoing auction on one side of the room, and in some parts, all you had to do was fill a form with the amount you would be donating.

Something caught Jessie's eye, and she came to a stop, forcing Seth to stop also. He looked at her with concern. "What is it?"

Jessie pointed at the thing that had caught her attention. It was a giant claw machine with various plushies inside. She had her eyes on a blue and white giant octopus plushie. She looked at Seth with puppy eyes. He looked back at her, confused. "What? What is it?"

Jessie pointed at the claw machine, and his eyebrows shot into the air. "You want to play with that? Right now? I don't even know why this is here. Come on. I need to see Mr. Ferguson."

She shook her head and refused to bulge. She could have just this one thing she wanted, at least for the day. Realizing she wasn't going to move from the spot, Seth rolled his eyes and walked to the claw machine. Jessie resisted the urge to squeal with excitement as she quickly followed him.

"What do you want?" Seth grabbed the handle controlling the claw.

"The blue and white unicorn." People paused to stare at them as Seth began to control the claw. A woman in a beige jumpsuit frowned at her husband. "Why can't you be this romantic?"

Seth concentrated on pulling out the plushie, but it kept falling. He hated losing because Jessie noticed how concentrated he became on getting the plushie out.

Jessie stood beside him and stared into the transparent box containing the plushies. "Oh, oh, that was close. Let me do it."

Seth shook his head and tried getting it again. Finally, the plushie fell into space outside the machine. A loud cheer jolted Jessie, and when she turned to look, a crowd of people had gathered around them and had been watching the entire process.

"Here you go." As Seth handed her the plushie, a flash went off, and Jessie turned to see that a camera was aimed at them. A couple of photographers aimed their cameras at them like a weapon and took numerous pictures of them. Jessie felt overwhelmed by the sudden paparazzi, and she blinked profusely. Seth put a hand to her waist and guided her away from the cameramen.

Jessie settled back into their seat, and Seth gave her a brief smile. "I'll be with Mr. Ferguson for some minutes, okay? You stay here. If there's anything you want, just wave at the waiters passing by." He left her and walked toward Mr. Ferguson, who was conversing with a group of men.

"What's your name?" Jessie whipped her head towards the person addressing her. It was the elderly woman that was sitting opposite her. Her husband must have left for some time because Jessie didn't notice she was there.

"Oh, I'm Morgan Chase." The elderly woman nodded slowly, still staring at Jessie in a way that made her feel awkward.

Finally, she spoke again. "He must like you a lot."

Jessie looked at her with confusion. "I don't understand?"

"Mr. Irving. You're his woman, aren't you?"

Jessie sat up and felt her cheeks heat up. "Oh er, yes I am."

"How long now?"

Jessie thought off the top of her head. "6 months now. We haven't been together for long yet."

The woman gave her first smile and nodded slowly. "It doesn't matter. He cares for you a lot. He hasn't seen anyone since... well, Annabelle."

Jessie wasn't sure what to say, so she just played with the tiny purse on her lap. The woman stood up and patted Jessie's hand. "Treat him well. That young man has been through a lot."

Soon, it was just Jessie at the table. She looked around and stared at the elites in the room. Some were already leaving to get ready for the reception. Jessie glanced at Seth and saw he was still in a conversation with Mr. Ferguson.

All of a sudden, she felt the hair on her skin rise, almost like someone had a piercing gaze on her. Jessie looked up and saw a man in a grey suit, standing all by himself. He looked at Jessie and gave her a creepy smile, his unusually sharp teeth glistened under the light. His dark hair was drawn into a low bun, and although handsome, Jessie found something unsettling about him. He held up his wine glass to Jessie before walking away.

She stared at his receding figure before he completely disappeared from her sight. A hand touched Jessie's shoulders, and she jolted. She turned to see who it was; it was Seth.

"Woah, are you okay?"

Jessie felt an overwhelming urge to hug him. It was inappropriate, but something about that man had scarred her deeply. Since she was sitting, she wrapped her arms around his torso and rested her head there. Seth leaned and said, "Oh good. I almost forgot people were still watching us. A display of affection will be good."

Jessie detached herself from him. Right, she almost forgot too that it was all a show.

Seth held a hand to her and assisted Jessie as she stood up. "Mr. Ferguson and his wife want to see you."

They walked up to Mr. Ferguson and his wife. Mrs. Ferguson was wearing a pink dress with a pink feathered hat and donned pink gloves. In her oversized purse, there was a tiny poodle with a giant pink bow around his neck. Everything was so...pink.

She beamed when she saw Jessie. "Oh, darling! You are the beauty that stole Mr. Irving's heart. You look amazing." Jessie instantly warmed up to her, and she returned the smile.

"Thank you. You look nice yourself."

Mrs. Ferguson blushed and laughed it off. "Oh, nonsense. How's the event? Have you been making friends?"

Jessie glanced around and watched the women quickly look away when she caught them staring. "Ah, well. Not really."

"They'll come around. They're just a little bit jealous."

Seth stretched his hands towards Mr. Ferguson. "Morgan, this is Mr. Ferguson. Mr. Ferguson, this is my, er, girlfriend, Morgan."

Mr. Ferguson grabbed Jessie's hand and shook them. "Nice to meet the woman who has won Mr. Irving's heart. How do you do?"

"Oh, I'm fine. And you, sir?"

Mr. Ferguson gave a loud laugh, and his belly jiggled beneath his tux jacket. "I'm doing great. Please call me Bill. I'm not that old."

"And call me Mary." Mrs. Ferguson piped in a while, patting her dog, which had started whining slowly. All of a sudden, the dog started yowling, drawing the attention of everyone to them.

"Oh, dear, shush, Lily!" Mary lifted the poodle out of her bag and rocked it like a baby, but it didn't work.

Jessie leaned over and watched the dog for some seconds. She could feel Seth's gaze on her back. "She seems to be afraid...by some sort of presence." Jessie straightened and looked around the room, but there was nothing out of the ordinary. She collected the dog from Mary and patted it continuously. "It's okay. You're safe. Nothing is wrong." And slowly, the dog went quiet.

Mary stared at her with awe, and Jeff guffawed and clapped. She turned to look at Seth, and he was watching her with a look she didn't recognize. The look you get when you open a mystery box, and you discover the unexpected. When the dog was completely calm, Jessie handed her over to Mary.

"Wow." She smiled at Jessie, the lines around her eyes creasing. "That was something. Are you a vet doctor? Seth never mentioned what you did."

"I'm a clea- er, I mean, I'm a schoolteacher. For a small school in London. Nothing much."

"That's nice. But you should consider doing something with animals. You're perfect."

Jessie smiled at the statement. Until her mother got better, she wouldn't be pursuing any dreams soon.

Mr. Ferguson patted Seth's shoulder. "The reception will begin in an hour. We should get ready. Mr. Irving, we'll finalize everything soon."

He shook Jessie and Mary gave her a tight hug, her tiny frame barely coming up to Jessie's shoulders. Together, they walked out of the building, and a bodyguard that had been stationed near the door followed them.

"Come on, let's-" Seth stopped his sentence mid-air and froze. He sniffed the air and cocked his head like he was listening for something. "Nah, not possible." He shook his head and turned to Jessie.

"Huh, what was that?" Seth gave her a small smile and shook his head at her question. "I thought I...it's not possible. Let's go."

Okay, Jessie thought. Now that's weird. They walked out of the event center, and Jessie was surprised to see that it was dark already. "What's the time?" She asked Seth.

He looked at his Rolex. "15 minutes past eight. Come on, let's get going."

Seth held open the door, and Jessie was about to get in when she caught a flash of the man in a grey tux that had creepily stared at her earlier. She glanced at Seth, and he was scanning the entire space, with a look of panic on his face. Jessie decided to brush it off. She looked around again, and there was nothing, just people entering their vehicles and leaving the venue.

Finally, Seth got into the driver seat and drove off. The entire journey was quiet, and the soft jazz music playing on the radio filled the silence. The distance was short because soon enough, they pulled into the driveway of a skyscraper hotel. The building towered into the sky and Jessie craned her neck to see the top.

She opened the door before Seth could open it, and he cocked his eyebrows. She avoided his gaze as she embarrassedly remembered how she felt about him. Who did the heck fall in love with someone out of their social status, a person who had been mean to her and was currently using her to score points with Mr. Ferguson, right? That was her.

Jessie felt anger well up in her stomach as she thought about the whole thing. She had only known him for weeks, and he didn't seem to be over the death of his wife. How could she do this? Fall for an emotionally unavailable man.

"Woah, slow down." Seth pulled her back to attention, and Jessie stumbled to a stop. She hadn't realized she was walking so far. She slowed down, and together, they entered the lobby of the hotel. One word Jessie could use to describe the hotel was clean. The dark tiles were clean that they shone with the reflections of the light. The walls have painted a combination of lilac and white, and those seemed to be the reoccurring colors in the entire space.

Multiple chandeliers hung from the cathedral-like ceiling, and Jessie had to squint to adjust to the sudden presence of so much light after being in the dim lighting of the Ferrari.

Seth walked up to the receptionist, who stood up when she saw him approach. "Mr. Irving! We have been expecting you. Welcome to Royals suites and hotels; here is the key to your room. This bellhop will escort you to your room. Please, enjoy your stay here."

Jessie noticed how the receptionist had ignored her all through. She peeped at the name tag on her blouse; Anna. Anna stared at Seth with stars in her eyes, and it was clear she was infatuated with him. Jessie felt jealousy stir in her, and that only made her feel angrier. *Seth isn't mine and will never be,* she reminded herself.

She walked away from the lobby and blinked back the tears in her eyes. Seth caught up with her. "Hey, is something wrong? If you're tired, it's okay. We can just skip the reception."

Jessie shook her head and gave him a watery smile. "Something got into my eyes. It's okay. Let's get this done." She made up her mind to keep the professional distance between them, after this, for her sake at least.

The Bellhop led them to the elevator, and they all got in. Jessie could see Seth staring at her quizzically out of her peripheral vision, but she looks straight, hoping the elevator journey wouldn't last too long. Finally, the door slid open. "This way, please."

The bellhop pointed into a long and well-lit corridor. The walls were painted a separate color from the lobby; it was a cream color with tiny flowers drawn into the paint.

"Here is your room. Enjoy your day." The bellhop turned to leave, but Seth pressed some bills into his hands. He beamed and bowed before walking away.

Chapter 9

As soon as Seth opened the room, a call came through on Jessie's phone' it was Amelia. "Hey, Amelia?"

"Hey! How are you and Mr. Irving doing?"

Jessie glanced at Seth, who walked into the room. "We're good."

"Okay. The makeup artist and stylist are already on their way so that you can get ready. Your clothes are in the bedroom, by the way. Oh, the media is having a FIELD DAY! You're their mystery girl, and don't forget to stick to the story. It'll all die down soon."

Jessie's heart raced faster. Was she in the tabloids already? "Oh, alright. Of course."

"Tell Mr. Irving I said hi! Bye." The conversation ended with a click, and Jessie turned to see what Seth was doing. He had left the living room and was inside the bedroom. The living room was classy in a way that reminded me you weren't home. The deep brown floor shone brightly and complimented the beige sofas that were professionally arranged. A television was placed on a vintage desk, and artificial flower vases were arranged on both sides.

It was beautiful but just wasn't... home. Jessie caught herself mid-thought. Wait, it was Seth's house, not hers. Her own home was a ratty apartment downtown Albany.

The bedroom door was open, so Jessie walked in. Seth had his bareback to her and had his pants on but was unfolding his shirt so he could wear. His back flexed with muscles as they were defined and firm.

The first thing Jessie noticed was how fit he looked. She had never seen him go to the gym, yet his muscles bulged. Then she noticed the multiple scars on his back. Some looked like claw marks, and others looked like teeth marks... extremely sharp teeth. There were puffed-up scars, jagged scars, tiny scars that had faded out with time.

Jessie hadn't known she had made a sound until Seth whipped his head towards her. He quickly wore his shirt, leaving the buttons undone. "Oh, hey."

Her cheeks heated up, and Jessie focused on any other thing but his bare chest. "Amelia says hi."

Seth buttoned his midnight black shirt, which he paired with grey pants. He didn't wear a jacket this time and looked more casual. He passed by her, and Jessie caught a whiff of his familiar woody scent. "I'll leave you to get ready. I'll be waiting in the living room."

Jessie nodded and turned to watch him shut the door behind him as he walked out of the room. She would have loved to take a shower, but there was no time, plus she didn't want to get her hair wet. Jessie unzipped the dress and folded it onto the bed. The gold dress was laid in a box with the top half-opened. Jessie brought it out and held it up, admiring how it sparkled under the light.

There was a zip by the side, so she unzipped it to make it easier for it to wear. She ran her hand down the dress, admiring how amazing it felt on her body. She then proceeded to zip it up, only for the zip to get stuck.

"Oh crap. Oh no." She pulled at the zip, but it wouldn't budge. "Lord, if this zipper spoils, I'm going to cry. I can't afford to damage this."

A loud bang at the entrance, and it was Seth knocking. "Is everything okay?"

Jessie slumped with embarrassment, but she knew she had no choice but to seek his help. "Er, not really. I need help.'

The door slid open, and Seth slowly walked in. "What is it- oh." He ran his gaze over her form as Jessie squirmed in the dress. He cleared his throat and went closer to her. "Looks like it got stuck to a piece of fabric. Hold on."

Jessie felt her heartbeat rapidly until it seemed like it would jump right out of her chest. She was so close to him that she could see the heart-shaped freckle on his cheek.

"There." The zipper was unstuck, and Seth slowly zipped the dress up. His hand lingered on her skin, and Jessie's knees became a week. She looked into his eyes and saw something else swimming in the blueness of them. Was he feeling what she was feeling?

Seth leaned closer, and Jessie's eyes widened when she realized what was about to open. She moved closer and shut her eyes slowly.

"Hi, I hope I'm not too late-Oh!" They both sprung apart at the sudden interruption. The makeup artist stood there with bulging eyes, and the stylist who had just joined her looked confused. The makeup artist stuttered. "I-I am so sorry to interrupt you."

"It's okay! He was just helping me fix my zipper." Jessie blurted out. She had a half desire for the ground to open up and swallow her. Seth avoided her gaze and walked out of the room. Jessie's heart broke a little, but she pushed the disappointment away and gave the makeup artist a shaky smile. "Shall we?"

The hairstylist worked on Jessie first. She curled Jessie's and pulled it into a chignon, with few curly strands purposely left out. The makeup artist went next, and Jessie kept avoiding her gaze. Finally, she cleared her throat. "I'm sorry I walked in on you like that."

Jessie blushed. "It's nothing we were just-"

"It's none of my business, and you don't have to explain. But something is going on. Why not make it exclusive?"

Jessie shook her hair, the curls bouncing on her face. "Nothing is going on. H-he doesn't feel that way."

The makeup artist looked at her with disbelief. "Do you see how that man looks at you? Girl... if anyone looked at me like that, I'll marry him. Anyway, all done."

Her words stayed with Jessie as the makeup artist packed her products. She didn't believe her; she imagined things. She wore her heels and grabbed a matching purse that was in the box with her dress. She was ready.

Jessie stepped out of the room and saw Seth watching TV. He sensed her presence and turned to look at her. Seth did a double-take, and his eyebrows flew up ad he took in Jessie's look.

"You, er, look... nice." Seth stood up from his seat. Jessie gave him a genuine smile and caught her reflection in the mirror. Pearl pins decorated her hair in strategic positions and shone when she moved under the light. Her dress sparkled under the light as she moved closer to him. She looks like a shiny star.

Seth held a hand out to her and led her out of the room. Jessie held on to his hand and basked in the comfort that he was doing this because he wanted to and not because people were around. The elevator ride was short, and Jessie received the shock of her life when the doors opened. A mob of paparazzi rushed at them, with Anna trying to hold them back.

Seth swore. "Shit! How did they get in here? Where's the security?"

Someone put a microphone in Jessie's face. "Are you Mr. Irving's rebound?"

Another one struggled and came forward. "How will you fill into Annabelle's shoes?"

"Do you think he genuinely loves you?"

"You're Mr. Irving's first woman in seven years since Annabelle; how do you feel?"

Seth growled and pulled Jessie towards him. He pushed through the crowd, and luckily, the manager came through with some security men. He managed to create enough space for them to get out of the lobby and to the car.

The short, balding manager was sweating profusely as he apologized. "I am so sorry. Ma'am, I hope you are okay?"

Jessie stared at him, dazed. The experience had shaken her up, and she didn't realize she was shaking until Seth took her hands and looked at her with concern. "Hey, are you cold? You're shaking."

Jessie opened her mouth to speak, but nothing came out. The manager looked at her with fear; she could make or break him if anything had gone wrong.

Seth pulled her into a hug, and she welcomed his warmth. He slowly rubbed her back. "You're hyperventilating. You don't have to go for this. I'll drop you home."

Jessie thought about the oppressive feeling she always seemed to have in her apartment and Jeff's snide comments, and she shook her head. She took deep breaths and said, "No. I'm okay. I was just caught off-guard for a bit. Let's go." She stepped out of the hug and immediately missed the feeling of his arms around her.

"Please, d-don't hold this against our hotel, Mr. Irving." The manager moved closer with a look of desperation on his face.

Seth dismissed him. "Whatever. Just get us out of here." The manager ran to the paparazzi and waved them away, pushing the guards on them. Seth opened the door for Jessie, and she got in, already familiar with the smell of leather. He got into the driver seat and revved out of the driveway and into the streets. It was a few minutes after 9 pm and everywhere was already dark.

Jessie closed her eyes for some seconds and savored the moment. It would all end in some hours' time, and she would be back to living her everyday life. So, she allowed herself to bask in temporary elegance. A song came on the radio, and Jessie swayed to it.

I'll always love you, whether or not you feel the same.

And I'll never forget you because you are a part of me.

And maybe you don't feel the same, and you don't see me the way I see you.

But it doesn't matter, because I love you.

She opened her eyes and whispered, "I love you."

The Ferrari pulled into the underground parking lot of an event center called Glass House. That was to be taken literally because the entire building was made of gold-colored glass. As the light hit the glass walls, the building shone and resembled a giant bulb. Jessie wondered if the building was bulletproof.

Seth opened the door for Jessie, and they walked out of the park and into the building together. It was a cocktail party, so everyone was standing and moving around. Again, they stopped to stare as soon as Jessie and Seth walked into the building. A woman nearby audibly said, "Wait, they're serious?" Jessie heard that and held Seth's hand. He wrapped his fingers around hers.

A woman in a silver dress sat by the corner and played a gigantic harp inside a transparent ball. Jessie wondered if she could breathe well in that.

A woman with boobs bulging out of her skin-tight dress sashayed to them. She put her hand on Seth's arm and purred. "Seth, darling. It has been a while. I see you brought a... friend."

Jessie refrained the need to roll her eyes and simply smiled at her. Seth pulled Jessie closer to him and said, "Hello, Helen. This is not my friend; Morgan is my girlfriend."

Helen looked at Jessie and gave her a fake smile. "Oh, hey there. I see you finally snagged Seth all to yourself. Not for long." She tsk-tsked and walked away.

Jessie was stunned by the audacity, and it was probably all over her face because Seth spoke to her next. "Don't listen to her. Helen has been trying to sink her claws into me for years now. It doesn't help that her father is a close friend of mine. Come on."

They moved towards the middle of the room, and soon, people started to look away from them. Jessie was glad for the sudden lack of interest. She couldn't imagine dealing with this every day. A server walked up to them with tall glasses of bubbly champagne. Seth took two glasses and handed one to Jessie. She took a sip and savored the superb taste in her mouth.

There was a buffet table just by the corner with all sorts of expensive meals. Jessie's stomach rumbled, and she realized that she hadn't eaten all day.

Seth chuckled when he heard her stomach rumble. "Let's go get something." They walked up to the buffet table, and Jessie scanned the menu that was beside the dishes.

She decided on a dish of Lobster with stuffed Rigatoni and carrot puree. Seth raised his eyebrows at her plate. "That's a good choice. I see you picked up some expensive tastes from me," he teased.

Jessie rolled her eyes. "Please, you eat microwaved food." She jokingly puffed her chest. "I learned this all by myself."

Seth let out a laugh that shocked Jessie. She had never heard him laugh before, and it was nice to hear the sound. A pregnant woman that was also serving herself grinned at them. "You are such a lovely couple."

Jessie opened her mouth to reply, but Seth beat her to it. "We truly are. Thank you." He looked at Jessie and gave her a genuine smile. She wasn't fully sure of what that meant, but she allowed the butterflies in her stomach to flutter freely.

"Now, where can I devour this unashamedly?" Jessie asked as she looked around the hall. Seth pointed at the corner where few empty chairs had been arranged. They walked towards the place and sat there. Jessie bit into the lobster and groaned. "This is so good."

Seth nodded. "Mr. Ferguson owns a chain of restaurants too. He always wants the best."

Jessie held up a forkful of food towards him. "Here. Aren't you hungry?"

Seth shrugged. "No, not really." Jessie looked at him doubtfully. This was someone that could devour all of this in one bite. She held up the fork again, and this time, Seth rolled his eyes and swallowed the meal. And that was how they ate the meal, with Jessie and feeding Seth part of the meal. He made jokes about being a billionaire, yet here he was, being spoon-fed by a cleaner. Jessie laughed till her cheeks hurt. For a moment, she forgot she was pretending in front of elites, and it was just them.

She shared stories of her childhood and watched Seth listen attentively. "Honestly, I never had many friends, but there was this girl; Emily. We became friends because we got paired for a biology project. We were cool until I found out she was using my locker to hide tadpoles."

Seth laughed. "No way."

"Oh yes. Imagine my shock when the janitor opened my locker because he heard some noises in there, only to find baby frogs."

"Wait, how didn't you know?"

Jessie dropped the empty plate. "My locker was always stuffed, so she hid the jar in the back."

Seth shook his head. "That's crazy." His eyes clouded. "I never really had a normal childhood. My father was a...different man, and my mother died when I was young." Jessie was afraid to move. Was Seth opening up to her? She kept quiet and listened. "I took responsibility quite early, so I never really did kid's stuff."

Jessie gave him a soft smile. "At least you turned out amazing." Seth looked away, and Jessie noticed his fists were clenched. If she hadn't been listening carefully, she would have missed him, saying, "I don't know about that."

"Ladies and gentlemen." It was Mary. She wore a long baby pink dress, and of course, her poodle was in her arms. "Please step onto the dancefloor." A violinist had joined the woman playing the harp, and a beautiful tune floated in the air. People walked onto the middle of the room that made up the dancefloor and moved slowly with their partners.

Seth stood up and stretched his hand towards Jessie and mock-bowed. "May I have this dance?"

Jessie smiled and played along. "Yes, you may." They walked up to the dance floor, and Jessie put her hands around his neck while Seth put his hands around her slender waist. They moved slowly to the music.

Seth whispered, "Have I told you how good you look today?"

Jessie leaned in and rested her head on his broad chest, and they swayed to the music. "I believe you have."

"Well, I'm repeating it." Jessie looked into his eyes, and for once, she was sure of what she wanted. She didn't know if she felt the same way or if he could even feel the same way, but she didn't care.

She wanted to kiss him so bad, so she did. Her knees almost gave way when she felt his warm and soft lips on hers, so Jessie tightened her hold on him. She could feel the soft tickle of his breath beneath her nose, hands softly holding her face, and he deepened the kiss. Jessie forgot she was in the middle of strangers, but one thing was sure. She liked Seth. Maybe... maybe even loved him. Out of breath, they slowly broke the kiss, and Seth rested his forehead on hers and breathed her in.

"Wow," Jessie said in a shaky voice.

Seth chuckled. "Yes, wow is the word." The music came to an end, and they slowly walked off the dance floor. Jessie stopped mid-step. "I need to use the bathroom."

Seth nodded. "Okay, I'm waiting for you."

Jessie walked out of the hall and asked a guard, "Please, where are the restrooms?"

He pointed at a separate building near the hall. She thanked him and briskly walked to it. The air was chilly, and Jessie suspected that it was nearing midnight, yet she wasn't sleepy. She thought about the kiss and did a little skip as she walked to the toilet. It felt magical.

She opened the door leading to the restrooms and entered the one with the 'female' sign. The cubicles were all empty, so she entered the first one and locked the door. She relieved herself and washed her hands when Mary ran into space, fear written all over her face.

"Morgan, oh my god. I-it's Seth. He's hurt."

Jessie felt her heart drop into an unseen hole. Her head swam as she moved closer to Mary. "What's wrong with Seth?"

Mary shook her head as tears swam in her eyes. "You should see for yourself. H-he's right at the back."

Jessie ran out of the restroom and into the driveway with Mary right behind her. She paused to look back at Mary. "Where exactly?" they had left the building and were in front of some empty shops. Mary pointed into a dark alley, and Jessie ran into it. She squinted into the dark space and called out. "Seth? Seth!" But no one answered.

She turned, "Mary were-. "A tall figure stood in the way, and Jessie's heart raced. "S-Seth, is that you?" the figure moved closer to her, and Jessie gasped when she saw who it was. It was the creepy man she had noticed watching her back at the event. He was still wearing his grey suit, but his shirt was unbuttoned.

Jessie took a step back. "Who are you? And where is Seth?"

The man laughed, and his voice sounded raspy. "I don't know if you have realized, but I'm not Seth. I'm Gavin."

"W-what do you want, and where is Mary?"

"Right here." Mary walked into the alley and gave a wicked smile at Jessie. "Oh honey, you are too gullible." She frowned at Gavin. "What are you chit-chatting about? Aren't you going to finish the work?"

Gavin smiled. "Of course, my darling. Give me a second." Jessie watched in horror as Gavin's bones painfully restructured themselves; still, he was bent in a crouch. She could hear his bones crack as they moved around. His legs twisted in inverse ways, and fur sprung out from his body. His mouth opened as his teeth became long and stained yellow canines. He let out a loud growl and proceeded towards Jessie.

Jessie screamed and ran blindly into the alley. She tripped over heels and removed them as she ran. She could hear Mary's gleeful laughter behind her. Jessie ran until she bumped into a wall; the alley had come to an end.

"No, no, please." Tears streamed down her face as she pawed the wall. She turned back and found a vast wolf standing in front of her. It was the wolf she had seen in front of Seth's house.

Its yellow eyes gleamed as saliva dripped from its teeth. Jessie picked up a stone and threw it at the wolf, but it kept progressing. She was hysterically crying and kept throwing stones at the wolf, but it was all flimsy.

All of a sudden, it sprung at Jessie and sank its teeth into her arm. She screamed and tried to push it off, but it only sank its teeth more. Blood drained from her arm, and Jessie felt her head spin. She slowly sank to the ground and felt her breathing go faint. Everything swam, and the pain was unbearable to the point that she began to pass out.

The last thing Jessie saw was something significant jump on the wolf. It was another wolf, and it roared as it took a swipe at Gavin, then everything went black.

Chapter 10

Jessie heard voices in her head as white light swam around. She opened her eyes slowly and gasped when a terrible migraine hit her.

"She's awake." She heard footsteps approach her. She tried to turn her head, but it felt too heavy for her to lift. Her throat was so dry it felt like sandpaper. Someone touched her face, and Jessie rolled her eyes to see who it was; Seth.

"Hey, how do you feel?" Seth looked awful. His eyes were puffed shut, and he had red marks all over his arms. Jessie tried to remember what had happened, but she couldn't remember. Mary... it had involved Mary. Suddenly, all the memories of last night came rushing back, and Jessie jerked up with wide eyes. "No, no, no!" She moved around and yanked out the IV attached to her wrist.

The doctor came running into the room and tried to calm Jessie down. "Woah, you need to relax, ma'am. You are safe here, and there is nothing to be afraid of."

Jessie couldn't hear him. All she could see were yellow eyes and sharp teeth dripping with saliva. She felt something pierce her, and soon, Jessie felt her eyes close slowly. As her eyes fluttered to sleep, she saw Seth look at her with guilt.

Jessie woke up again and saw that the day had passed so quickly. She didn't feel as weak as before, and she looked around. She was in Seth's bedroom, and the clock said it was 4 pm. She felt some pain in her right hand, and when she looked at it, her wrist was heavily bandaged. It seemed the doctor had left because the house sounded empty. Jessie wondered if he asked questions as to how she got the wound.

Someone stirred beside her, and Jessie turned to see Seth sleeping. His eyes were moving under his eyelids like he was distraught even in his slumber. She watched his long eyelashes cast tiny shadows on his face and how his plump lips were slightly parted in his sleep.

She rolled over and went over last night's occurrence. A wolf had attacked her. No. She had been attacked by Gavin, who turned into a wolf. Jessie rubbed her face; she was going crazy.

It wasn't real, she said to herself. But she stared at her arm, blood sipping through the bandage, and deep down, she knew it had happened. There was no logical reason for it, but it had happened.

She was so thirsty. Jessie slowly sat up and groaned when dark spots danced in her vision. She stood up and swayed on her feet.

"Woah." Seth caught Jessie before she fell to the ground. "You need to stay in bed." She hadn't even heard him get out of bed. She gave him a grateful smile for catching her.

He looked at her with concern. "What do you need?"

"Water."

He carefully led her back to the bed and opened a small fridge in the corner of his room. He brought out a bottle of water and opened the cover before handing it to Jessie. The bed dipped as he sat beside her. Jessie gulped the water and sighed with relief as the patch in her throat disappeared. She dropped the empty bottle and lay back on the bed. She wondered what she looked like, but she knew she must look awful.

They were silent for some seconds before Jessie spoke. "That was you, wasn't it? The other wolf."

Seth glanced at her before reluctantly nodding. Jessie let out a breath. She was trying to stay calm but inside, she was freaking out. She breathed in the smell of the black sweatshirt and sweatpants she was wearing. They were Seth's. She wondered how more of his clothes she would have to wear.

"So, you were the wolf I mistook as a dog that night. The night I finished my last day at Jerry's."

Once again, Seth nodded. He rubbed his face, and Jessie noticed the stress lines on his forehead.

"I think you owe me an explanation."

Seth opened his mouth to speak, but it came out as a croak, so he tried again. "I-I'm a wolf shifter. My mother was human, but my father...not so much. Gavin and his pack killed Annabelle-that was my wife."

Jessie's heart raced. "You mean there are more?"

"More than you think, but Gavin is out to get me. He's out for blood. He wants everything I want, and if he can't get it, then he ruins it."

Jessie wasn't sure what her heart was racing for. The fact that Seth wanted her or that her life was in danger. "What do you owe him?"

Seth stood up and walked to the window. His frame looked slumped, and Jessie badly wanted to go and soothe him. But she was afraid of him. She was almost surprised when he finally spoke. "Because Gavin is my twin brother, and he wants everything I want."

Jessie blinked rapidly at the revelation. "So you're a wolf, and your brother, who is a wolf, is trying to kill me, to spite you. Siblings squabble, right."

Seth walked up to her with a troubled look on his face. "This is not a joke. Gavin is trying to kill you."

"And why can't you kill him first?"

Seth rubbed his head and paced around. "It's not that simple. If I kill Gavin, his pack will come after you, and they will kill you. The only thing to do is to take over, and I can't do that because... I'm an outcast."

"Outcast? Why?" Jessie didn't fall under any of it, but she wanted to get all the information she could get.

"I... I killed my father." His voice cracked at the end, and Seth slumped on the bed with defeat. Jessie had had it. There was no way she could deal with any of this. "I don't want any of this."

"You're already involved and-"

"I don't care!" Seth was taken aback by her outburst. "You have lied to me from the onset. Tell me, why exactly did you hire me? You just happened to be the stranger I bumped into, and a few days later, you're my new boss!"

Seth opened and shut his mouth. "I can't explain any of it now, but I promise I will-"

"I quit. I can't do this." Jessie felt angry tears pool in her eyes as she felt betrayed. She stood up rapidly and swayed again. Seth tried to help her, but she shoves him away. "Don't touch me! I'm leaving."

"Jess, it's dangerous. Gavin is still out there. I only managed to injure him, but he'll be back for you."

Jessie whipped her head and felt tears fall from her eyes. "I'll rather be out there than right here with you. You have been lying to me all this while."

Seth took a step back as hurt reflected in his eyes. He turned away from her. "You can leave. Amelia will send in your last paycheck."

Jessie silently cried harder at the finality in his tone. She walked out of the room and ran out of the house.

"Open!" She furiously banged on the gate till the gate automatically slid open. Jessie wiped her tears as she walked up the hill leading to the main road.

"Taxi!" A yellow car screeched to a stop at her yell. She got in and put a hand to her mouth to stop herself from crying harder. She gave him her address when he asked and turned to look out the window.

The driver looked at her through the rear-view mirror, and his eyes widened. "You're the lady, all over the internet. Seth Irving's girlfriend is in my car. Madea will never believe this."

Jessie frowned at him in confusion. What did he mean all over the internet? She brought out her phone from her tote bag and realized it had been switched off. When Jessie switched it on, notifications trickled in, and her phone wouldn't stop pinging.

There were two texts from Lucy.

Hey! I'm free today; wanna hang? Mia misses you.

Jess? You're all over the blogs! What's going on?

She had more texts from unknown numbers and even one from Mina - *Hey, you're dating your boss? That was quick! I love that for you.*

Her phone rang, and when Jessie checked to see who it was, it was an unknown number. She picked it. "Hello?"

"Hi! Miss Jessie, this is Dave from Entertainment Action, and we want to confirm if-"

Jessie hung up and put the phone on her chest. Another call came through, and it was also an unknown number. How did they find her number? Her eyes widened when she realized what had just happened. The blogger had called her by her real name. How did they quickly find out?

"Crap." She groaned and put her head on her lap.

The cab driver glanced at her again. "Is everything okay, miss?"

Jessie sighed. "Yes, yes, it is."

They rounded the corner leading to her apartment, and Jessie gasped at the sight. There were news trucks, journalists, and cameramen right in front of her apartment. "Stop!"

The cab came to a sudden stop. "Woah! What's the problem?"

Jessie ignored him and groaned again. There was no way she could get into her apartment peacefully. Jeff will sell her out at any chance he gets; she shouldn't risk it.

She decided to call the person that may be able to help her. After two rings, Lucy picked up. "Hey! Where have you been?"

"I can't explain now, but I need your help. My house is...currently unavailable, and I'm afraid to check into a hotel because they may easily find me there."

"Oh honey, of course! I'm about to finish my shift at the hospital. Meet me there. I'll be done in 20."

Jessie sighed with relief. "Thank you so much, Lucy. I appreciate this."

"Of course! It's nothing. See you then, bye." The conversation ended with a click.

Jessie leaned towards the driver. "Back out of place and take me to St James hospital. I'll increase your bill. I expect you to keep my location a secret, yes?"

The driver swallowed and threw his hand in the air as he reversed the car. "I promise!"

St James's journey wasn't long, partly because the driver knew a shortcut and because Jessie pushed him to drive faster. She didn't want the media to catch up with her if they find out she wouldn't be coming home.

She wondered why they hadn't bothered checking Seth's house. After all, she had just left the place.

Jessie didn't know she had spoken that aloud until the driver replied, "I'm surprised you don't know this. Everyone knows that the paparazzi have been banned from going to Seth Irving's home. They harassed him and came up with different theories that he had a hand in his wife's death. It was all doubtful because even a child knew how much he adored his wife. Poor thing."

Jessie clammed at the thought of him. She didn't want to think about any of it because it still didn't make sense to her. One thing was sure; he had lied to her and put her in line of danger. Whether or not he did that purposely didn't matter now; she needed to stay away.

The cab halted in front of St James, and Jessie paid the cabman. She narrowed her eyes and spoke to him. "I have your plate number taken down. You mustn't tell anyone where I am."

"Hey! I promise. Can I go now?" Jessie got down and watched the car speed away. She felt a pang of guilt for threatening him like that, but she didn't just want the paparazzi not to know where she was. Jessie was also hiding from Gavin. She tried to persuade herself that it had all been a hallucination, but one look at her arm, and she remembers that it truly happened. A man had turned into a wolf and had attacked her.

Chapter 11

Jessie shivered and threw on the hood of the sweatshirt she was still wearing. She ignored the fact that it was Seth's and walked into the hospital. Jessie sat in the waiting room and hid her face behind a random pregnancy pamphlet. Luckily for her, Lucy came into the waiting room and scanned the place. Jessie gave her a quick wave and gestured 'outside' as she stood up and walked out of the room.

A few seconds later, lucy came to join her. "Woah! What happened to your hand?"

Jessie sighed and shook her head. "it's a long story, but I'll tell you everything when we get out of here."

Lucy led the way to the parking lot. "Come on, let's pick Mia and Aaron from school before we head home."

Jessie got into the SUV, and Lucy backed out of the parking lot. For the first time all day, Jessie felt a little bit at ease.

Lucy looked at her with concern. "You have been crying. Your eyes are swollen and red. Are you okay?"

Jessie considered lying, but the weight of everything came crashing on her. She put her face in her hands and moaned. "I am not okay. I can't believe any of this is happening right now. It's not safe to talk about it now but, when we get to your house, I'll tell you everything."

Lucy nodded and looked back at the road. "You looked happy."

Jessie looked at her with confusion, so she clarified. "I mean with your boss. Your pictures are slapped all over magazine covers and tv shows; I'm surprised we aren't bombarded with paparazzi."

"Trust me, I was. I narrowly avoided them. How did they find my address?"

Lucy laughed. "It's the media, and they can find anything. And um, there's a little bit of a scandal."

Jessie's heart raced faster as her eyes got bigger. "Wait, what?"

"My phone is in my bag. Check my saved articles."

Jessie dug her hand into Lucy's purse and brought out her phone. She scrolled and found the saved articles. She saw the one she was finding because her heart dropped immediately she saw the headline.

What is Seth Irving Hiding?

Check out his new woman, whom he introduced as Morgan, but Jessie Lewis, a former worker at Jerry's Coffee Point. This unknown woman followed billionaire and young business mogul Seth Irving to Bill Ferguson's annual charity event.

Much attention is on this mystery woman because she is the first woman to be seen with Mr. Irving officially. But here's the thing, with a little bit of digging, we discovered that this woman is not a school teacher in London as she claimed, but Mr. Irving's cleaner!

Love can be found anywhere, but a billionaire dating a cleaner? Now that is something. Stay tuned to Entertainment Action for more juicy gossip on this topic!

Jessie closed the article and stared into space. "This is bad."

Lucy looked at her with curiosity. "Not that bad, but why did you lie?"

"Seth-I mean, Mr. Irving wanted me to. He was looking for someone to take as his date, and apparently, it was important he went with someone."

They pulled up into the parking lot of Mia's elementary school. Lucy looked at her with doubt. "So none of it was real?"

The memory of Seth's lips on hers flashed through Jessie's mind, but she shook it away. "Yeah, it was fake."

Lucy turned off the ignition and sat in the car for some time. "Don't worry about it. It will all die down soon, and everything will be back to normal. Are you going back to work there?"

Jessie looked at the children filtering out of the building as the school bell rang. "I'll start looking for a new job."

At least she had enough to keep her mom in the hospital for the next few months. She wished she would get better.

"Alright, gotta go get Mia. I'll be back."

Lucy got out of the car and walked towards the school building. Jessie brought out her phone and dialed her mother's number. She usually wasn't strong enough to pick calls, but Jessie decided to give it a try.

She had almost hung up when her mother's voice sounded through the speakers. "Jessie?"

"Hey, mom. How are you doing? How's your health now."

"I'm much better. Jessie, why are you on TV? There's some news going around about you and-"

'Mom, it's nothing. I-er just went for some event with my boss."

"Are you dating your boss?" Jessie heard amusement creep into her mother's voice. "Is my little Jessie coming out of her shell?"

Jessie rolled her eyes. "Mom, I'm not dating my boss. I simply escorted him to an event."

Hannah snickered over the phone. "Didn't look that way to me."

Jessie huffed, but deep down, she felt relieved. Her mother sounded better, and she made a mental note to visit her soon. Maybe she could find another job and save enough for them to go on that vacation.

"Anyway, mom, I gotta go. Make sure you aren't watching TV all day."

Although she couldn't see her, Jessie could imagine her mom rolling her eyes. "I'm not a child. See me soon, Jessie."

Jessie bit her lip as she felt a pang of guilt. "I will, mom. I promise." She looked out the window and saw Jessie and Mia walk up to them. She cocked a brow at Mia's purple tutu. "Alright, mom, gotta go. I love you."

"Love you too."

Mia jumped up when she saw Jessie and ran towards the car. Jessie opened the passenger door and crouched with her arms wide open. "Hey, you! Loving the outfit."

Mia grinned, and Jessie noticed that she was missing two teeth. "Thank you! I miss you." It came out as "I mish", but it warmed Jessie's heart.

She gave her another hug. "I miss you too, Mia. Come on, let's go get Aaron." Lucy smiled at them and got Mia into her booster seat before revving out of the parking lot.

Mia was very chatty. "Mom, I made a new friend today. Her name is Lily, like the flower! She likes SpongeBob, too. She might be my best friend."

Lucy grinned at Mia through the mirror. "But what about Bobo? I thought Bobo was your best friend. Aaron, too."

Jessie turned and watched with amusement as Mia frowned, then smiled again. "Bobo is my doggy best friend! And Aaron will be my boy's best friend. I can have more than one best friend."

Jessie smiled and clapped. "Wow, that's clever of you, Mia."

The little girl beamed, but her expression changed when she set her gaze on Jessie's wrist. "What happened to you?"

Jessie made eye contact with Lucy and turned her attention back to Mia. She gave her a reassuring smile. "I just had a little accident."

Mia looked at her doubtfully. "That doesn't sound little." Jessie glanced at her bandaged arm and was alarmed that it was still bleeding. Blood had seeped entirely through the material and was now spreading.

She forcefully smiled to reassure Mia. "Trust me, I'm okay."

Luckily, Lucy came to her rescue. "Okay, Mia, that's enough questions for today."

They pulled in front of Aaron's middle school, and they didn't have to spend much time because Aaron was waiting outside the school. He walked up to the car and slammed the door close.

"Woah." Lucy turned to look at him. "Someone's got an attitude today. What's wrong?"

Aaron noticed Jessie, and she smiled at him. He scowled and looked back at his mom. Yikes.

"Next week is Bring Your Dad to School." Aaron frowned at his mother.

Lucy looked away uncomfortably and drove away from the school. "Why is there such a thing? I can always-"

"No!" Everyone, including Mia, was startled at his sudden outburst.

Lucy's lips quivered, but she stood her ground. "Young man, don't use that tone on me."

Aaron sulked but didn't say anything after that. The car ride was quiet, and Jessie felt like she was intruding. So, she whispered to Lucy. "I think I can just stay in a hotel or-"

Lucy pursed her lips and shook her head. "No, no. It's no big deal at all. Aaron is... in one of his moods."

The Toyota came to a stop in front of a small house. Regardless of the size, it was quite homely and welcoming. A small but dainty garden decorated the house's entrance, and peonies and dandelions danced peacefully in the warm breeze.

Lucy unlocked Mia's booster seat and dropped her onto the floor. Aaron didn't wait for anyone before he stormed to the door. When he turned the handle and realized it was locked, he simply stood by the door and sulked.

Lucy sighed and rolled her eyes before smiling at Jessie. "Welcome to our home."

"It's stunning and seems cozy." It was the truth. Jessie liked it already. Lucy walked up to the door and unlocked it with her key. Jessie followed behind her and walked into a small but airy living room. Lucy switched on the light, and it revealed the translucent curtains that she pulled apart. The entire living room was painted in a mint green tint that contributed to the room's brightness and airiness.

"So, what would you like to eat, guys?" Lucy sat down and massaged her feet. Even though she had a smile on her face, she looked exhausted. Jessie suspected she had had a long shift.

Jessie dropped her purse on the couch and decided to offer her help. "How about I cook something for all of us."

Lucy shook her head, red curls escaping her bun. "Oh no. you're my guest."

"No, it's wonderful. You should rest or do any other thing."

Lucy wouldn't back down. "How about we all just order Chinese?"

"Okay, but I'm paying."

"But-"

Jessie shook her head. She was never someone to leach off another person. Jessie lifted her hands in surrender and nodded.

Mia jumped up and down. "I want to make the order."

At that moment, Bobo ran into the living room and barked with delight when he saw Jessie. He jumped on her, and Jessie laughed as he coated her face with Saliva. "Hey, you. I miss you too." She checked his foot, and it was completely healed.

Jessie grinned at Mia. "I see you took good care of him. Good job!"

Mia did a twirl and jumped up. She had a lot of energy for someone who had had a busy day in school. Aaron ran up the stairs and slammed his bedroom door.

Lucy sighed and held Mia's hands. "Come on, Let's go take a shower. Jessie, you can stay in the third room at the end of the hallway.

Jessie climbed up the stairs and walked into the hallway.

The wallpaper was patterned with tiny oranges and bananas. It gave the space a festive feel. She could hear Lucy and Mia laughing behind a door that she assumed was the bathroom.

The room at the end of the hallway was unlocked, so she just opened the door. It revealed a tiny bedroom with a single bed in the room. The curtains were pulled apart, and it looked like it doubled as storage because she could see empty boxes piled in a corner.

It wasn't much, but she was grateful to have a place to stay. Jessie sat on the bed and stared at her arm. The event of the past few days came rushing back, and Jessie shuddered. All of her sudden, her head spun, and everything went blurry. She had a splitting headache when her vision came back.

"What the heck was that?" She held her hurting head in her hands. Slowly, the pain faded away. Jessie unwrapped the bandage and stared at the vast bleeding gash in her hand. The bite marks had cut deep into her flesh, and some chunks of flesh had to be sewn together. Still, it bled. Jessie helplessly stared as droplets of blood trickled from her wound.

A knock at the door startled her before Jessie realized it was Lucy. "Come in."

Lucy walked in and gulped when she saw her hand. "What in the world happened to your hand. Oh my god, let me get my first aid kit."

She ran back downstairs, and Jessie turned back to staring at her hand. The skin around her wound was turning dark, and she wondered if the doctor couldn't do anything about it. Why was it this way? She closed her eyes, and yellow eyes and snarling teeth flashed in her head.

Jessie gasped and opened her eyes just as Lucy entered the room. She held a small red box and sat on the bed next to Jessie.

"Let me see." Jessie handed her hand to Lucy, and she winced as Lucy applied light pressure to the skin around it. "It's inflated. Seems like it has been treated recently?"

Jessie nodded. "It was treated this morning."

"The dressing is still okay, but for some reason, it is still bleeding. I'll clean it up and apply some ointment around the area; hopefully, it reduces the swelling." She opened the box and brought out cotton swabs and methylated spirit to keep the wound clean.

Jessie hissed at the sting of the antiseptic but was glad that she could at least keep it clean. After gently applying the ointment, Lucy wrapped her hand in a new bandage. The wound was still bleeding, but Jessie was glad that it felt much better, at least.

Lucy patted her. "There you go. Now take a shower; the order will soon arrive. I'll leave out some clothes for you to wear. They may be a bit short, but they'll do."

"Thank you," Jessie said. Lucy smiled at her and walked out of the room. Jessie looked down at the sweats she had been wearing. It faintly smelled of Seth, and Jessie couldn't help but worry about him. He had been wounded too.

She shook her head. It was none of her business anymore.

She left the room and walked into the bathroom. It was only a little bit bigger than her bathroom back in her apartment. She could still smell the orange bathing gel that Mia had used, and the bathtub was still wet. Jessie stripped and got into the bathtub. She laughed to herself when she realized she had spent more time in other people's bathrooms than hers in the past few weeks.

The water was warm, yet Jessie felt feverish. The chill seemed to be coming from within, but she got out of the bathtub anyway. There was a towel on an iron robe, and she wrapped it around herself before walking back to the room.

As promised, lucy had dropped a pair of shorts and a plain T-shirt. The shorts were shorter than they should have been, but the shirt was fine. The extensions were still in her hair, so she just brushed it down and plaited it into a messy braid. She stared at her face in the small hand mirror that was on top of a box. There was a red wound on her forehead, but it was slowly healing. She had bags under her eyes, and Jessie decided to sleep better, at least.

The doorbell chimed, and Jessie looked for her purse before walking down the stairs; the order had arrived. She quickly handed him the money for the Chinese food and collected the pack.

"Thank you." Lucy smiled at her as she set the dining table. She looked up to the stairs and yelled, "Aaron! The food is here. Either you come downstairs, or you don't eat tonight."

For some seconds, there was only silence, and Jessie decided he wasn't going to come downstairs. A door slammed close, and soon, Aaron came downstairs. He was still sulking, but at least he wouldn't miss dinner.

They sat down and munched on their meals at the dining table. Lucy looked at her children. "Kids, tell Miss Jessie thank you."

Mia, sweet as always, shouted, "Thank you! I hope you will live with us." Aaron pursed his lips but muttered a barely audible "Thank you."

Jessie grinned at both of them. "You are welcome."

Soon, they were done with the meals, and Lucy threw away the empty packs. "Kids, go do your homework. Call me if you need any help."

Aaron ran up the stairs without answering her. Mia gave them both sweet hugs before walking to her room, Bobo trailing right behind her.

"Your kids are so sweet," Jessie said, and she meant it. While Aaron may be a little bit closed off, it was clear he loved and respected his mother no matter what.

Lucy shrugged. "I try. It has been hard, to be honest."

"I can see that." They settled into a comfortable silence before Jessie decided to speak again. "I suppose you have some questions you will like to ask."

Lucy hesitated. "I'll prefer if you just narrate what happened."

Lucy closed her eyes and leaned her head back against the dining chair. "My boss needed my help, and I decided to assist him. He needed to finalize a deal with Mr. Ferguson, and apparently, he had to go with someone with whom he was in a relationship. His assistant forgot to remind him about the event till the last minute, and I was their only choice."

Lucy nodded to show that she was paying attention. "But what about your wound?"

Jessie stared at Lucy and thought about how hard she had worked to get to where she was now. There was no way she would get Lucy and her kids in something as dangerous as this. So, she came to the truth as close as she could afford. "Oh, that. Some dog attacked me."

Lucy's eyes widened. "those bite marks are deep. That must have been a huge dog. I hope you got a shot for rabies, though. Lord knows what those animals carry these days."

Jessie thought about it and decided that must have been one of the first things the doctor had done for her, so she nodded.

Lucy sighed with relief. "That's better. But why did you quit?"

Jessie opened her mouth to formulate another lie, but she suddenly felt tired. She wanted to say something true, at least. "Mr. Irving and I... We kissed, and things just got awkward."

Lucy's eyes widened. "Woah. So you do have a crush on him?" Jessie wanted to tell her how 'crush' was an understatement, but she nodded in response.

"I guess I didn't want to get involved in his life. His wife died some years ago, but he doesn't seem to be over her."

Lucy frowned. "Didn't he kiss you back?"

"Oh, he did."

"So why do you think he isn't over her?" Jessie looked up at Lucy in surprise as she asked the question.

"Because he was mean to me when I first started walking with him."

"Is he still mean to you?"

Jessie hesitated and thought about the time he had cleaned up her knife cut. The time he allowed her to sleep in and offered her his clothes. "Well, no but-"

"Oh, Jess. You're quite clueless for someone your age. Just from the way he looked at you in the pictures, it is clear that this man adores you. Of course, things won't be as straightforward as they should be. You are probably the first woman he had had genuine feelings for since his wife."

Jessie shook her head and told Lucy about how he admitted to putting her life in danger, but she knew she couldn't do it. "You don't understand. No way can happen."

Lucy stared at Jessie with such a piercing gaze that she looked away. "Jess, what are you so afraid of? Why do you think you are unlovable?"

Jessie opened and closed her mouth, but nothing would come out. She could only listen as Lucy continued. "You are running away from something you want so much. Listen, before I realized my husband was a total jerk, I remember having a massive crush on him before we got to know each other appropriately. He would sit by the fountain every evening with a book in his hands. I would peep at him and run away when he turned to look at me. Finally, I summoned the courage to let him know how I truly felt."

She sighed. "It didn't work out the way I hoped for it to, but I'm glad I finally took the step. I would have never known if he liked me back or not had it been that I kept my feelings to myself. You need to stop assuming and take action."

Jessie allowed the words to sink in as she stared out of the window and into the orange sunset sky. It didn't matter if she was right or not; she couldn't go back to him. She couldn't bear to think about him without remembering he was a werewolf and was Gavin's brother, the one that had tried to kill her.

She shook her head, and Lucy sighed. 'Well, I tried my best. You might as well continue this way. I'm going to check up on the kids, okay?" Lucy patted her shoulder and walked out of the room.

Jessie sat all by herself at the dining table and stared into space. Could Lucy be correct, though? Was she pushing Seth away because she didn't believe he could love her? She shook her head. No. that wasn't why. He had lied to her, and he was too dangerous for her. Staying away was the best thing.

Although it was just evening, Jessie felt her eyes get heavy. She had had a long day and wasn't fully recovered yet. She climbed up the stairs and into the room she was staying.

She laid on the bed and stared at her mobile phone that she had switched off. She wondered if Amelia had heard Jessie quitted. She was going to miss Amelia for sure; she had been nice to Jessie from day one.

Jessie was counting the columns in the ceiling when her eyes fluttered close. Jessie was back in the alley, and she was running. She struggled to move, but it felt like she was running through a river of mud. Her movement was slow, and Jessie felt the frustration of the entire situation.

She looked behind her and saw Mary laugh hysterically. "You can run, but you can't hide. Seth will be mine." Mary grew and grew into a huge giant, her heels trying to crush Jessie.

She managed to dodge her and ran ahead to meet Gavin as a giant wolf with saliva dripping from his teeth and his hungry yellow eyes fixated on her. His mouth parted into an evil grin as the wolf spoke.

"Little lamb, you will be mine. I will make you mine, whether alive or dead."

He was about to pounce on her when another wolf appeared out of nowhere and attacked Gavin. They rolled over each other with growls and snarls piercing the air. Gavin threw it into the wall with one enormous swipe at the other wolf, and it crashed with a whimper. Jessie tried to run to it, but she was so slow. She yelled into the air. "Seth... Seth... Seth!"

Jessie opened her eyes with a loud gasp as she scanned the room with horror. She slowly calmed down when she realized it was just a dream. She groaned, "Oh, thank God. It was just a dream."

She noticed that sunlight had brightened the room, and she wondered how long she was asleep. Her eyes widened when she checked the time on the clock; it was few minutes to 9 am. Why the heck had she slept for that long, yet it only felt like it had been few minutes?

She stood up and walked down the stairs. The smell of fried eggs and bacon was in the air, and Jessie's stomach growled. She felt sick and famished at the same time. Jessie walked into the kitchen and saw Lucy stirring something on the food.

Lucy turned and smiled when she saw it was Jessie. "You are finally awake. You were knocked out yesterday."

Jessie rubbed her eyes. "Yeah. I'm surprised I slept for that long. I never really sleep for so long."

"Well, it's good. It is probably your body trying to heal." Lucy dished the bacon and eggs into two plates and slid one to Jessie over the counter.

Jessie smiled at her gratefully. "Thank you very much. I'm guessing the kids are in school?"

Lucy nodded as she bit a piece of bacon. She was in blue scrubs and seemed to be heading to the hospital already. "Yup. I'm about leaving for work now, so make yourself comfortable at home."

Jessie shook her head. "Nah. I'll be stepping out in search of a new job."

Lucy frowned at her. "Shouldn't you be resting? You look so pale."

Jessie self-consciously touched her face, but she was relentless. "Nah, I need to go out."

"Okay then. Just don't stress yourself. Also, you can put the key under the flower pot in front of the door. The kids may get home before you."

Jessie hesitated but decided to ask, "How's Aaron now?"

Lucy sighed and slumped against the kitchen counter. "He's still in a mood. I'm not sure what to do. He has to bring someone for career day, and it has to be a man. How sexist."

Jessie pondered on how she could help. "Wait, it just has to be a man, right?"

Lucy nodded slowly. "Yes, but I can't talk to the doctors at the hospital. I'm not so close to any of them, and they're always so busy."

Jessie knew someone who she could talk to. Hopefully, he would listen to her. "I-I may have someone who can help."

Lucy looked at her doubtfully. "Are you sure?"

"No, I'm not, but I will ask."

Lucy smiled at her and hugged her. "Thank you so much. I have to go now, or I would be late."

Jessie waved at Lucy as she left for her shift at the hospital. She munched on her bacon and thought about the dream she had had. Although there were loopholes and she couldn't entirely remember the story, Jessie remembered the details of the dream, and she shivered as she remembered how real it had felt.

She dropped the empty plate in the dishwasher and headed back upstairs. The black sweats she had arrived in were washed and folded on the bed. Jessie walked to the bathroom and rinsed her mouth with peppermint mouthwash. She got into the bathtub and hurriedly took a shower. As she wore the sweats, she realized Seth's smell was gone and now replaced by the scent of freshly washed clothes.

"I hope those people have left. I need to go back home." She murmured to herself as she turned on her phone. The cellphone chimed as notifications streamed in. There were three missed calls from Amelia. Jessie wasn't sure how she would face her, so she just ignored them. The others were unknown numbers, and she suspected they were from the media houses. There was no missed call from Seth.

"No." She shook the thought out of her head. "He doesn't matter anymore." Jessie grabbed her tote bag and walked out of the house. She wished she had a pair of sunglasses, but she decided to make do with putting the hood over her head.

Jessie thought about going home first, but she decided to do that later. To make sure the paparazzi were gone by the time she got back. Her phone rang, and she checked who it was. It was Jeff.

She rolled her eyes but picked the call. "Hello, Jeff."

He ignored her greetings and went straight to the point. "Where are you?"

Jessie almost laughed at the absurdity of the question. Jeff had never asked about her whereabouts unless, of course, he was going to gain something from it. So, she decided to lead him on a wild goose chase.

"Oh, I'm actually at Hexagon hotel." This was a hotel that was right on the outskirts of town. Jessie hoped the paparazzi would learn to leave her alone. Plus, she couldn't pass an opportunity to make Jeff look like a fool.

She could hear the smirk creep into his voice. "Okay, bye." And he hung up.

"Serves him right," Jessie muttered as she waved down a cab. "Cleveland Avenue."

The driver was a grumpy old man, and Jessie was glad he didn't pay her any attention. She wasn't sure who may recognize her anyway. Her heart raced faster as she got closer to the house. What if Seth didn't want to see her? She couldn't force him anyway. Jessie was so deep in thought that she was jolted back to reality when the car came to a stop in front of the gate leading to the mansion.

She paid him and watched the cab zoom away. As she walked towards the house, Jessie rehearsed what she'd say, but everything sounded wrong.

"I need your help- Nah. That sounded too somehow. Would you come to a kid's- oh dear? This is harder than I thought." She arrived in front of the familiar mansion and pushed the intercom. It was silent for some seconds, and Jessie considered turning away, but soon, the gate slid open.

Jessie walked to the door, and she was about to push the button when the door sprang open. And there was Seth, standing and staring at her with an expressionless look on his face. Jessie opened her mouth to speak, but nothing came out.

She tried again. "C-can I come in?"

Seth said nothing but stepped aside. He walked up the stairs, and Jessie followed him, determined to speak to him. He entered his study and sat behind an enormous mahogany desk. Jessie noticed how his wounds had healed completely and wondered if that was an advantage of being a shifter. She scanned his face for any hint that he was what he had confessed to being, but Seth looked as regular and usual as he always did.

He ignored her and flipped through some files on his desk. Jessie swallowed her pride and spoke first. "You owe me a favor."

That caught his attention because Seth looked up at her in confusion. Jessie quickly continued not to lose him. "I mean for following you to the event. I'll like for you to return the favor."

Seth remained silent for some seconds, then he spoke. "What is it?"

"I want you to come for my friend's kid's career day."

Seth stared at her as if unsure whether or not she was joking. "I don't understand?"

Jessie shrugged and spread her hands. "That's it. I need you to come for Aaron's career day."

He stood up from his chair and walked up to Jessie. She took two steps backward as he approached her. He kept coming closer, and she kept moving back until she hit the wall behind her. He placed both his hands at each of her sides and leaned in. Jessie thought her heart would jump out of her chest and land on the floor with a plop.

"So, you have a chance to ask me for anything, and you choose to ask for someone else?" Jessie almost forgot to reply as she got lost in his blue eyes. How was she going to forget him when she kept being drawn back to him?

"Y-yes."

He leaned in and placed his lips on her cheek. "I missed you. I hate that I got you into this, but I don't know why I can't stay away."

Jessie hated that he had such an effect on her. She leaned her cheek against his and felt his stubble on her skin. She sighed, "I'm supposed to hate you for getting me into this. I'm trying to hate you, but it's not working."

Seth looked into her eyes and leaned in for a kiss. Jessie gasped as her lips touched his warm ones. She hadn't known how much she was craving his touch, and now that he was, she felt electrified. She felt his tongue tease her, and she grabbed onto his neck as her knees went week.

Seth lifted her against the wall and held onto her thighs as he kisses her passionately. He came up for air and nibbled on the side of her neck. Jessie gasped at the unexpectedly pleasant sensation of it.

He carried her out of the room and up into his bedroom, kissing her like he couldn't get enough of her lips. Jessie's head hit the soft bed, and she already missed the presence of his lips. He traced his lips from her neck down to her stomach and nibbled on her navel. Jessie held back a moan as he softly on her stomach. She removed the sweatshirt and was about to pull down her sweatpants when he shook his head.

"No, let me." He slowly pulled off her sweatpants and kissed her thigh. He chuckled at her SpongeBob patterned underwear, and Jessie's cheeks flamed up. "Hey, this is my favorite underwear."

"I see that." He moved up and unhooked her bra, revealing nipples that desired to be touched. He placed his lips on one nipple, and Jessie moaned with pleasure. He moved to the second one and rolled his tongue on her warm breasts.

He put a hand into her underwear, and Jessie jerked with pleasure as his fingers moved rhythmically inside her. He kissed her as his thumb circled against her. Jessie's legs stiffened as she ground against his hand. She felt her eyes roll to the back of her head, and she is pushed to climax. With a moan of his name, Jessie came onto his hands.

When the feeling subsided, she put her hands to her eyes with embarrassment. She wasn't a virgin, but it had been a while since she had sex with any man. Seth removed her hands from her eyes as he stared at her with wonder. "That's probably the hottest thing I've ever seen. Please don't be shy."

With that, he kissed her again, and Jessie allowed herself to bask in the unique feeling of his body against hers. He removed his shirt to reveal his well-carved body. Jessie leaned over and slowly removed his jeans. Gently, he pushed her back onto the bed as he kissed her again. He withdrew and looked at her. "Can I?"

At that point, Jessie didn't want anything else, so she nodded and spread her legs for him. Her eyes widened at the size of him. "There's no way that will fit."

Seth slowly slid his member into her, and Jessie gasped at the pressure of it. Slowly, he began to move, and she adjusted to the feeling of him in her.

"I want you." He whispered as he pumped into her faster. As they moved into a rhythmic tempo, Seth clapped his hands with Jessie's, and she clamped her legs around his waist. Together, they melted into each other.

Seth kissed her on the lips as they separated. "Be mine." Jessie only smiled before her eyes fluttered close, and she soon fell into a deep sleep in his arms.

Chapter 12

When Jessie woke up, it was a few minutes after 9 pm. She turned to look at Seth, who was in a deep sleep. His eyes twitched beneath his eyelids, but he didn't seem like he would be waking up anytime soon. She thought about what had just happened and blushed. She didn't regret it, but she felt a little self-conscious. She didn't know how she ended up falling for him, but her heart raced each time she saw him.

She wanted to be with him, but Jessie felt all the years of doubt rise in her. Why would he want to be with her? She stared at him and felt tears well up in her eyes. He deserved someone better. Someone who could fit into the large shoes Annabelle had left behind.

She quietly stood up and dressed. With one last look, she walked out of the bedroom. Luckily, the front door wasn't locked so that she could sneak out of the house undetected.

She cringed when the robotic voice sounded but hoped Seth wouldn't wake up. She ran till she got to the road.

She hadn't thought it all through because few cars were passing by. Thankfully, she saw a yellow cab approach and quickly waved it down.

Jessie got into the back seat, relieved, and turned to bring out her purse in her bag. "Whew, thank God. I thought I'd never find a cab."

"You're welcome, Miss Jessie." Jessie's head whipped up in a flash as the voice registered in her head. No, it couldn't be. How did he find her?

Gavin looked back at her and grinned. "Well, hello again."

Jessie felt her throat seize up, and she opened her mouth in a scream. All of a sudden, she felt Gavin's fist hit her face, and everything went black.

Jessie opened her eyes to the cold water being poured over her head. She gasped at the sudden shock of the cold liquid down her back. She coughed and tried to move but realized she had been tied to a tree. She pulled against the strong rope, but it wouldn't budge. It was very dark around her, but the moon provided a little bit of light.

Jessie turned her head around and realized she was in a forest. Giant trees surrounded her, and she was tied to one. She struggled with the rope, but nothing happened.

"Helppppp!" She screamed till her throat was hoarse, and her voice cracked. She heard a snap from behind her, and she struggled to turn her head, but she couldn't.

"Who's there?" She felt so much fear that tears started rolling down her face. She sobbed harder when she heard another snap to her left. One by one, different men came out of the woods and surrounded them.

She didn't recognize any of them. Some were short, some were tall, but they all looked powerful.

"Well, well, well, is this not our little princess." Gavin walked out of the trees and crouched in front of her. He raised a hand to Jessie's face, and she flinched, but he only wiped her tears. He stood up and spoke to the men who gathered around her. They were about ten of them, and Jessie feared that there might be more in the thickets of the forest.

"We have here, our beloved bait. Please, do not touch her, or you shall face the consequences." Gavin talked calmly, but everyone could hear the threat in his voice.

Jessie summoned the courage to speak. "What do you want from me? You already hurt me so much!"

Gavin frowned and looked at her bandaged wrist. "Hmm, I didn't realize it was this bad. Mary wanted you to be hurt. That woman's obsession with Seth is...something." He suddenly smiled and clapped. "Anyway, it will heal completely in two weeks. You'll be fine. That's if, of course, you leave this place alive."

Jessie's heart hammered as she struggled harder with the rope, but it only dug painfully into her rib. Gavin laughed at her attempt. "It'll take more than that to free yourself. You know, this makes me nostalgic. Only some years ago, Annabelle was in this situation. Poor thing, I told her not to run. Oh well."

Jessie's blood ran cold, and she realized how evil Gavin was. "You are so vile. Annabelle was pregnant. You monster!"

Gavin frowned at her like she was a schoolchild who had done something wrong. "Tsk tsk, shouldn't you be happy? If Annabelle weren't dead, you wouldn't be with Seth, would you?"

Flashes of her limbs tangled with Seth's ran through her head, and Jessie felt overwhelming shame and embarrassment. As if reading her mind, Gavin grinned and sat on a tree trunk. "You know, Seth should be thanking me. After all, he found his mate. Lucky bastard. Two mates in a lifetime."

Jessie shook her head and tried to adjust her body to be more comfortable. "W-what are you talking about?"

All the men around her snickered like she was left out of an inside joke. A large burly man chewing on a twig sneered at Jessie. "He didn't tell you? That you are his mate. Do you think you got the job by chance? Even we knew." The other men burst into laughter at Jessie's shocked expression.

She ignored them and turned to Gavin. "What did he mean by that?"

Gavin shrugged. "Well, Larry already answered you. You always know your mate, whether human or not. Why else do you think he picked you? Trust me; you're not so qualified."

Jessie ignored the sharp stab at her ego. "How do you know all this?"

"I know everything, Jessie. Everything."

Suddenly, someone yelled, "He's here!"

Gavin flew up from his seat and clapped with glee, his teeth gleaming in the darkness. "That was fast." He turned to Jessie. "You know, he didn't arrive in time for Annabelle. I suppose he has learned his lesson.

The trees shook as something charged towards them. The men all began their change as Jessie watched their bones painfully reconstruct and fur sprouting all over them. Finally, ten wolves stood in the clearing, baring their teeth.

A familiar wolf jumped into the clearing and growled loudly. Jessie knew it was Seth and more tears dripped down her face. Why did he have to come? It was one against ten wolves.

"Ah, brother. It has been a while. I see you have healed properly." Gavin grinned as if nothing was out of place. Seth bared his teeth in reply and the other wolves slowly advanced.

Gavin waved them off. "No, no. This is my brother. He can't hurt me. You are finally here since you killed dad."

Jessie watched Seth shrink back a little at the mention of their father. Gavin turned to look at Jessie. "You know, Seth is quite the character. He had a little disagreement with father, and next thing, he killed him." Gavin's expression turned cold. "And that is why I killed Anna."

Seth froze as he fixed his yellow eyes on Gavin. He slowly changed back to human and slumped to the floor. He was naked, but he barely registered that. His eyes were wide and fixated on Gavin. "No. You didn't."

Gavin stopped smiling, and little by little, Jessie noticed the cold creeping into his voice again. "Oh yes, I did. Did it hurt you? Well, that's how I felt when you killed father."

Jessie watched helplessly, and tears rolled down Seth's face with anguish. His voice cracked as he spoke. "How could you? She was carrying my baby. You killed my baby. You're my brother."

Gavin showed no signs of remorse as he beckoned to two wolves. "Seize him."

The two wolves slowly transformed back to naked men, and they lifted Seth by his arms. He didn't even put up a fight and allowed himself to be tied to the same tree as Jessie, their backs to the trunk of the tree. She heard Seth silently crying, and her heart broke for him.

Gavin clapped and smiled again as nothing had happened. "Well, boy, we'll figure out what to do with them later. You all should watch them." He walked up to Seth and spat into his face. "Don't even think of trying anything. I will rip both you and Jessie apart. Goodnight." With that, he walked back into the thickets of the forest. The two men wore their clothes and sat on a large rock, focusing their gaze on Jessie and Seth.

The remaining wolves paced around them, baring their razor-sharp teeth occasionally. Jessie wished she could turn to see Seth, but there was no way. She whispered, "Are you okay?"

She didn't get any response, but this did not dampen her. "Seth? Why are you here."

After some seconds, he said in a hoarse voice. "For you. I received a piece of your cloth with blood on it, and I knew they had had you."

Jessie grimaced at the thought of where they had gotten the blood from, but she looked at the sleeve of her sweatshirt; part of it had been ripped off. She opened and closed her mouth, unsure about how to bring the topic up. "I'm so sorry about Annabelle."

Seth gave bitter laughter. "She didn't deserve it. Fuck, I failed her."

"You didn't know Seth."

But he wasn't listening. He was trapped in his guilt. "They sent me a message. I simply thought it meant nothing. She was supposed to be visiting her mother and-" His voice broke at the end, and he hung his head, defeated.

"It's your fault."

Jessie heard his head whip up in a flash. "What?"

"It is your fault Anna died. Isn't that what you want to hear?"

"Jessie, please-"

"If you aren't going to fight for your life, fine. But I'm going to fight for mine. Would you rather dwell on the what-ifs or forgive yourself? Remember, you didn't kill her; Gavin did."

Seth kept quiet for some seconds, then spoke. "Okay, listen," He stopped to look around, to see if any of the men were eavesdropping. None of them seemed to be, but he whispered anyway, "if I transform again, I'm not sure how long I'll last in my shifter form. But I'll try my best to keep them off. Now, do you have anything silver on you?"

Jessie frowned. "Silver?" She shook her chest to see if she could still feel her necklace around her neck. There was nothing. "No. I think they took all my jewelry."

"Crap, crap, crap."

Jessie sighed in frustration before something suddenly popped into her head. "Wait." She whispered. "I can feel a pain in my head. It's one of the ones the hairstylist used."

"Oh great. It can only catch him off guard, and he'll switch to his human form for few seconds, but I hope it works. In ten seconds, we move."

Jessie counted in her head, and as soon as the ten seconds were up, Seth transformed back into a wolf. He roared and tore through the rope binding him to the tree. The other werewolves charged at him immediately. Seth was more significant than they were, but then wolves were more extensive in number. They all pounced at him and sank their teeth into his flesh. Jessie struggled with the rope and watched with horror as Seth was buried under the wolves.

Unexpectedly, Seth burst out and flung the wolves in a different direction. With one swipe, he tore through the rope binding, Jessie. She hurriedly stood up and immediately crashed to the ground. Her legs had been bound for so long that the blood there had stopped flowing correctly.

A wolf growled as it approached her; Jessie quickly stood up again and ran, with the wolf charging her. She tripped over a branch and turned to see the wolf jump on her. Out of nowhere, Seth pounced on the wolf and flung him aside.

Gavin rushed into the clearing and frowned at the scene. "I only took a nap for few minutes. Seems like I need to handle things now." Gavin shifted into his wolf form and paced around Seth. He didn't want to hurt his brother, but he was also pacing around Gavin. The wolves around them growled, waiting for Gavin's permission to feast on them.

Jessie looked around fervently, but luckily, none of them paid attention to her. Gavin pounced first. He growled as he held onto Seth's limb furiously. Seth howled with pain and kicked him away. He pounced again, and this time, the two wolves tumbled as they tore at each other. Jessie was horrified as she watched Gavin tear out a massive chunk of skin from Seth's hind leg. He bit into his back and howled with pain.

Jessie realized one thing, Seth was losing. Gavin swiped at Seth, and he kept moving backward till he stumbled on a jutting root. That was the distraction Gavin needed. Gavin sank his canines into Seth's back with one jump, and Seth sank to the floor.

"No!" Jessie ran towards Gavin and blindly pushed at the wolf, only to be flung away. All the air left her body as she heard the sickening crunch of her arm lying under her at a grotesque angle. Hot tears ran down her dirty face, and when she tried to move her arm, she screamed with agony.

Gavin approached her and placed a mighty paw on her chest.

He opened his jaws wide and imitated a grin.

Jessie freed her excellent arm and quickly stuck the hairpin into his paw. For a second, nothing happened. Then the smell of burning flesh hit her as Gavin slowly transformed into a human.

He screamed and squirmed on the floor as he held his foot. Jessie saw Seth fly into the air and pounced on Gavin from the corner of her eye, slashing across his chest. Gavin looked at the bleeding wound in surprise before falling to the floor, gasping.

Seth transformed back to human and held his brother's head, weeping. "I am so sorry."

Gavin only stared at him with glassy eyes, his breathing becoming labored. Seth continued. "I never told you. I couldn't have told you. I killed dad because he murdered mom."

Jessie's heart broke as she saw him cry harder.

"I saw him kill her, Gavin. We were only ten, and I couldn't do anything. I never told you because he would have killed you too. I swore to take revenge when I got older. I should have told you."

Gavin's face contorted with pain. "Why didn't you tell me this? What have I done?"

Seth didn't say anything but cried into his brother's shoulder. The other wolves advanced onto him, but Gavin weakly held up a hand, forcing them to stop. "Seth is your new Alpha. I hand over all my powers and responsibilities."

The wolves turned their heads to each other, then lowered their bodies to Seth.

He ignored them, his eyes on his twin brother. Tears rolled down Gavin's face. "I am so sorry. I can't believe I-I...How could I? God, I was so angry, I ruined everything for you."

Seth looked at his brother. "I want to hate you. For taking Annabelle from me." He glanced at Jessie. "For almost taking Jessie from me, but I can't. You're my brother, and I love you."

Gavin gave the first genuine smile Jessie had ever seen, and then, his eyes glowed brightly and slowly, the light went out like a flame put off by a breeze. Went glassy as he took his last breath. Seth buried his head in his brother's neck and cried harder. Jessie slowly walked up to him. Unsure of what to do, she knelt and put a hand on his neck. Seth hugged her and cried even more. Her heart broke for him, and she cried with him.

She looked at Gavin's lifeless body, and even though he had tried to kill her, she felt an overwhelming pity for him. To live with so much anger directed at your brother, to the point that you want to ruin everything for him, must be hard.

Seth composed himself and stood up to face the pack of wolves. Jessie felt a bit awkward because he was naked, but he stood with authority, and she ignored it. "Gavin passed the position of Alpha to me. Brothers, do you accept me as your leader?"

The wolves all howled to the wind and bowed their heads in agreement. Seth nodded. "I promise to do my best and never let you down. But anyone who touches a hair on Jessie's head, you will have to deal with me. My brother will be buried right here. Tomorrow, I shall plant a tree on his burial ground."

The wolves picked a spot and started digging out with their claws. Seth turned to Jessie and frowned at her broken arm. "Let's get you out of here." He transformed again into a wolf, which seemed to take a toll on him because he stumbled on his feet.

"Woah, are you okay? We can just walk." Jessie said to him. He nudged her and arched his back. Jessie sighed and sat on him. Seth bounded out of the clearing and tore into the trees. Jessie wrapped her excellent hand around his torso in terror. She didn't want to be thrown off his back.

Finally, they burst out into an unfamiliar road but kept to the side of the road. The streets were empty as it was past midnight, but they didn't want to take the chance of being seen by anyone. Jessie almost laughed at the idea of someone seeing a woman riding a giant dog.

Her eyelids felt heavy as the wind rushed past her face. She gently placed her head on his back as Seth bounced towards home. Jessie hadn't known she fell asleep until Seth nudged her. She opened her eyes and saw that they were in front of the gate.

He tilted his head towards the gate. She pushed the button and sighed with relief as the intercom recognized her fingerprint. It didn't look like Seth had any energy to turn back to human.

Together, they slowly approached the door, and Jessie pushed it through. She stared at the stairs and decided she had no energy to climb all the way.

Seth wobbled and fell to the ground. Jessie rushed to him. "Are you okay? What's going on?"

His eyes had rolled to the back of his head, and his tongue hung out of his mouth. Jessie looked around and quickly walked to the kitchen. She took out a bowl and quickly filled it with water.

She ran back to Seth and placed the bowl of water in front of him. He lapped it up so quickly that he almost choked.

"Calm down." Jessie patted his fur. Her eyes widened when she saw that he finished the bowl of water. He was still exhausted, but he looked better. Jessie stared at her broken hand and tried to move it. She howled with pain and decided she would deal with it first thing tomorrow. She gently set her hand on the ground and laid on the rug.

Seth placed his head on her belly and looked at her with his beautiful blue eyes. Jessie gave him a small smile. "It's never going to be easy with you, will it?"

He didn't answer because next thing, his eyes fluttered close, and he dozed off. Exhausted and battered, Jessie followed right after.

Chapter 13

It was noon when Jessie opened her eyes to see the doctor who had attended to her when Gavin had attacked her after the party, wrapping up her heavily bandaged arm. It was in a sling, and he carefully rested it on her chest. Jessie looked at him as he quietly picked up his things.

"How long have you been Seth's doctor? "Jessie asked him. He paused and blinked at her as if surprised to be spoken to.

"Ever since he was a little boy. I'm his mother's brother." Jessie's eyebrows shot up at the new revelation.

"Wow. I didn't know that."

He zipped his briefcase. "I don't expect you to know. Seth got into trouble a lot as a little boy. I have been caring him for a very long time now. There's only a little I can do since his wounds mend themselves."

"So, you know? That he's..."

The doctor nodded. "That he's a shifter? I know." He hesitated but added, "Annabelle never knew."

A comfortable silence fell between them, and she was glad she got some answers to her questions. "Thank you."

He bowed a little and walked out of the room. Jessie looked at the room she was in. It was Seth's bedroom, and she wondered how she had gotten there again. She touched her face and felt a Band-Aid on her forehead.

It was a cut she hadn't even known she had. Jessie was about to stand up when Seth walked into the room. He had red marks on his arms, but it looked like most of his wounds had healed. He wore a polo and shorts, exposing the gash on his leg.

Jessie pointed at it. "Why hasn't that healed?"

He sat on the bed and held her hand. "It'll heal. It's an intense wound and will take some time before it seals up. Now, how are you feeling?"

Jessie looked at him. His stubble had grown into a trim beard, and his hair stuck up in different directions. She held back a giggle because it made him look like a child. "Well, not too bad. Considering werewolves kidnapped me."

He pouted at her. "So was I."

Jessie laughed then sobered up. "I'm sorry about Gavin."

Seth turned his head away, a faraway look in his eyes. "It's okay. He's resting now."

Jessie looked at her outfit. She was wearing his oversized hoodie, the one he had told her not to wear. "Seth?"

He looked at her with concern. "What's wrong?"

Jessie shook her head. "Nothing. But I have some questions to ask, and you have to answer them honestly."

He stood up straight and nodded. "Okay."

"First of all, why do you pay $30,000 for a cleaning job? That's a huge amount of money."

Seth gave a small sigh and moved onto the bed, lying beside her. "My mom used to be a cleaner before she met my dad. She was betrothed to him, and her parents collected some money in exchange for her hand in marriage. I feel if she had been earning enough to run away, she wouldn't have married that man. I guess this is just my way of honoring her."

Jessie nodded slowly. "What kind of man was your father?"

Seth's face darkened. "He was a sick piece of shit. I didn't know he was beating my mom till I got older and understood the bruises she always had. My mother tried to protect us from him, so she lied to my father a lot. Gavin adored him, so he never realized. He killed my mother in a fit of rage. He dared to crush her tiny frame to death. Even after his death, I hate him."

Jessie held his hand. He was shaking with anger. Seth closed his eyes and slowly calmed down. She put her head on his shoulder. "I am so sorry."

"It's okay. Keep asking questions."

Jessie hesitated before asking her next question. She didn't know if it was time to ask. "Are you over, Annabelle?"

Seth was quiet for a long time, and Jessie's face heated up with embarrassment. She opened her mouth to express regret, but he spoke. "Annabelle was a light in my life. I had so much to deal with, and she was like a breath of fresh air. Her death devastated me, and it will always haunt me that my baby never lived to see me."

Jessie's heart broke, but she understood. He loved Annabelle, and she couldn't compete. She decided there and then to stay out of his life so that she could move on.

Seth turned to look at her, and he put a hand to her cheek. "But you... I don't understand you. I don't understand how a woman came into my life and has such a hold on you. I can't stop thinking about you, Jessie. I have tried, but you are like a scent that would leave. Your touch lingers even when you are gone."

A tear rolled down Jessie's face as she leaned into his touch. "Oh, Seth."

"So please, give this broken man a chance. I want to be with you properly. I don't want to be with Morgan or with my cleaner; I want Jessie Lewis, my mate."

Jessie stared at him and remembered Gavin's words about how she was his mate. "Did you know from the start? That I would be?"

Seth nodded. "The first time Amelia sent the names of those applying for the job, and I saw your name, I just knew. I really can't explain it, but I knew it was you. I was so scared of falling again that the constant thought of you pissed me off. I couldn't stay away from you, but I also didn't want to be near you."

He opened and closed his mouth, then rubbed his head with embarrassment. "I have a confession."

Jessie looked at him curiously. "What is it?"

"I didn't need a date for the fundraising event. I just wanted you to come with me."

Jessie gasped and sat up. "Amelia was in on this too?"

Seth laughed. "Oh yes."

"Would you look at that? A billionaire couldn't ask his cleaner to be his date for an event, so he made up a story." Jessie laughed as Seth's face turned red.

"You already disliked me, which is well justified by the way. I wasn't sure how you'd take it."

Jessie touched Seth's face. "I would have said yes." It was true. She wasn't sure when she started falling for Seth, but if he had asked her, she would have said yes.

He leaned in and kissed her deeply. "I want to be with you. What do you think?"

Jessie smiled against his lips. "I want to be with you, Seth. I want to learn everything about you. What you like, what you dislike."

Seth kissed her once again and stood up. "So, what will you like to eat?"

"Ooh, you'll cook for me?"

He rubbed his head sheepishly. "Well, I can microwave. Does that count?"

Jessie laughed and shook her head. "That's fine."

He walked out of the room, and Jessie smiled at his receding figure. She screamed silently into her pillow. She couldn't believe it. So, she had almost gotten mauled by wolves, and here she was, with someone she loved.

Wait, Jessie thought. *Loved?* She wasn't ready to admit that. She snuggled in the warmth of the duvet and inhaled Seth's scent. It seemed to be in everything he touched, and she couldn't get enough of his woody scent.

Not long after he left, Seth walked back into the room with a piece of toast and a cup of cocoa. He beamed as he placed the tray on her bed. "I made this myself."

Jessie grinned and clapped her good hand to her thigh. "Good job."

Seth held up a piece of toast to her mouth and fed her. Jessie tried to ignore the butterflies in her stories, but damn, it was the entire zoo.

Her phone rang all of a sudden. She was surprised that the battery had even lasted so long. It was on the shelf beside the bed, and Seth helped her reach for it.

Jessie picked up without looking at the name as she chewed her toast. "Hello?"

An unfamiliar voice came on. "Hi, Miss Lewis. Doctor Lucas told me to call you. You have to come to the hospital right now; your mother had a sudden brain failure."

Jessie's ears rang as she froze. The person at the end of the call said, "Hello? Are you there?"

Jessie took a deep breath and answered in a shaky voice. "I'm on my way."

"Alright, miss, please hurry."

Jessie stared at the disconnected phone as she tried to process what had happened. Seth looked at her worriedly. "Hey, what's wrong?"

She tried to speak, but her throat clutched up. Jessie quickly got out of bed but swayed at the sudden rush of blood to her head.

"Woah." Seth held her up. "You know what? Let's go together. To wherever it is."

She was finally able to speak, but tears fell from her eyes. "My mom. She h-had a heart attack. On my God, please no."

"Breathe. Come on, let's go." Seth lifted Jessie into his arms and climbed down the stairs. He picked up a car key from its position on a wall on walked into the driveway. He placed Jessie in an Audi and quickly backed out of the gate.

Jessie was numb. She didn't know how she described the hospital to him, but she did. No, not her mom. She couldn't afford to lose her mother; she was all she got.

As soon as they pulled up in front of the hospital, Jessie burst out of the car and ran into the building with Seth right behind her.

"Where is she?" Jessie screamed at the nurse she saw.

"Miss, you need to calm down. There-"

Jessie held on to her arm. "Please, I just want to see her."

The nurse tried to calm her down. "She is in the emergency ward. Please, you have to stay calm."

Seth held Jessie's hands and looked into her eyes. "Jessie, please, you're not going to help if you keep panicking. I need you to breathe. Take deep breaths with me, okay?" Jessie mimicked Seth as he took deep breaths, and she felt herself calm down.

They sat in the waiting room, and Jessie resisted the urge to pace around. She placed her head on Seth's shoulders, and he patted her. "Everything will be alright."

She wrapped her arms around him. "Thank you."

"For what?"

"For being here. I don't think I could have gone through this all by myself."

Seth kissed her hair. "It's okay. I want to be here."

The day went by, and the only time Seth left her side was to use the restroom and get donuts for them.

"I'm not hungry." Jessie knew her eyes were swollen from crying, and she felt embarrassed that she looked that way in front of him.

"Well, if you don't eat, you'll end up on a hospital bed. Come on, these donuts look good."

On cue, Jessie's stomach rumbled, and Seth shot her an 'I told you so' look. Sighing, she collected the donut and bit into it. She couldn't taste anything, but she ate it anyway. He had gotten them water, too, so she used it to wash down the meal.

"Thank you." She was grateful he was here.

Seth frowned. "You need to stop thanking me for things like this. I am supposed to do them."

Jessie was about to reply when she saw Doctor Lucas come their way. She flew up from her seat and rushed to him.

"Oh my God, how is she?"

She saw him frown at her arm in a sling but responded to her. "She's in critical condition. We've been monitoring her for weeks because she was getting better, but the relapse is sudden. She will pull through, but she needs to be under strict watch." He looked at her then shook his head. "I'm sorry, but this sudden development will attract some extra costs. Your mother doesn't have any health insurance, and I'm afraid you will have to pay for this."

Chapter 14

Jessie calculated the money she had in her account and realized everything would have to go to her mother's healthcare. She nodded. "Okay, I have some money I can deposit and-"

"I'll pay." Jessie's head turned to look at Seth. He ignored her and spoke to the doctor. "Please forward all the costs to me. I will pay everything needed to be paid."

"Seth, please, this is not your burden. I can always find a job and-"

Seth shook his head. "Jess, allow me to do this. Think of it as a payment for everything." Doctor Lucas looked back and forth as they bickered. Jessie opened her mouth to argue again, but Seth shook his head. "I don't want to hear it."

"Seth, it's a lot of money. I can't let you do that."

"You're not letting me do anything. I'm doing this because I want to." He turned to Doctor Lucas. "Please, make sure Ms. Lewis receives the best care, or I will be moving her."

Doctor Lucas shuffled uncomfortably on his feet as he nodded quickly. "Of course, we'll do our best." He shook Seth's hand and patted Jessie awkwardly before walking away.

Jessie turned to look at Seth. "What did you do that for? I could have handled it." She was mad at him. Jessie didn't know why, but she was used to dealing with her issues all by herself and didn't like feeling indebted.

Seth sat down and sighed. "Jessie, I did this because I wanted to. I'm not saying you couldn't have handled it; I just wanted to help."

"I'm not some charity case, Seth!" The nurse at the reception scowled at her. She reduced her voice. "You can't just treat me like I'm incapable."

Seth gritted his teeth. "I'm doing this because I love you. Damn, you're so stubborn." Jessie blinked rapidly, trying to process what she had just heard. Had Seth just told her that he loved her?

She stood there, still trying to process it. Seth stood up and held her hands. "Listen, it took me a while to get over Annabelle. I was so mean to everyone who worked with me, and I regret that. But you, I love you, Jessie. And I'm doing this because I want to."

Jessie leaned in, and she softly cried. "I can't believe how lucky I am."

He chuckled as he held her in his hands. "No, I'm the lucky one."

The nurse at the reception dropped the phone. "Miss Jessie, you can now see your mother." She glanced at Seth, and her eyes widened when she recognized him. "And um, I don't think you can take him with you. I'm sorry."

"It's okay." Seth kissed her forehead. "You can go. I'll wait here for you."

Jessie nodded and walked away from him. The hallway leading to the room where her mother had been put in was quiet. She opened the door of the room and saw a nurse with her mother. She quietly spoke to Jessie. "Please, try to stay as quiet as possible."

Jessie nodded and sat in the chair by the bed. Various things were hooked to her mother, and Jessie thought about how she looked like a machine. Hannah laid on the bed, and Jessie would have thought she was lifeless if not for the sound of the monitor hooked to her.

Her head had been shaved again, and Jessie knew she wouldn't be too happy about that. Her skin was the color of grey clay, and new wrinkles lined her skin.

"I love you, mom." It didn't matter if she couldn't hear her; Jessie wanted to say it. "And I want you to get better quickly, please." She stared at her mother, hoping for a reaction, but she got nothing. Defeated, she slumped in her seat and stared for some minutes.

Jessie stood up and kissed her mother on the cheek before leaving the room. She walked back to the waiting room, where Seth was still sitting. He stood up when he saw her. "How is she?"

Jessie shook her head. "Still the same."

"Stay with me, Jessie. I can't allow you to stay all by yourself." Jessie wanted to argue, but he was right. She didn't want to spend the night all by herself, in her tiny apartment.

"I'll have to get my things. I don't have any clothes."

Seth teased. "You're wearing clothes right now, aren't you?"

Jessie appreciated that he was trying to lift her mood, so she cracked a tired smile.

"Come on, let's go to your apartment." Seth guided her out of the hospital and got into the car. They drove out of the parking lot and into the main road. Jessie gave him the directions, and soon, they were right outside the apartment building. Seth got down and observed the building. "It's uh, it's... something."

Jessie rolled her eyes and walked into the building. It was just her luck that she bumped into Jeff on the way. He grabbed her arm. "How dare you lie to me? Huh? Do you-"

He didn't get to finish his sentence because Seth detached his hand from Lizzie's. Seth smiled at him, but it wasn't a friendly smile. "Why are you touching her?"

Jeff's eyes widened as he realized who it was. His voice shook as he spoke. "Mr. Irving, I-I'm so s-sorry, I didn't mean-"

Seth cut him off and turned to Jessie. "We're moving all your stuff tonight. If we can't get them all, I'll get someone to move them." It was clear he was refraining himself from throwing a punch at Jeff.

Jessie nodded and walked up to her room. As they climbed the stairs, she could hear Jeff cuss behind her. Good riddance.

She unlocked the door and walked into space. Although she had been gone for a little while, she could now see her room in a different light. She noticed the cracks in the wall, the fraying edges of her rug, and the faded wallpaper. She hadn't realized that her home wasn't so cozy anymore.

Seth looked around. "It's cute."

"I guess. I'm going to get my stuff in the room."

Seth nodded and sat on her favorite sofa. "Okay."

Jessie walked into her bedroom and switched on the light. The curtains were shut tight, but it wouldn't have mattered if she pulled them apart; it was late at night.

She didn't have many clothes anyway so that she could fit it all into a traveling bag. Jessie grabbed her plushie in one arm and looked around for what else she could carry. She fit all her shoes in a plastic bag and walked out of the room. Seth lifted a brow at her luggage. "That's all?"

Jessie shrugged. "That's all that I can take. Come on, let's get out of here."

He stood up and walked out of her room. As she followed him, Jessie turned back to look at her dim apartment. She hoped that would be the last time she'd see it and shut the room behind her.

Thankfully, she didn't meet anyone else on the road. Jessie wasn't sure she felt like talking to anyone.

Seth opened the door for her, and she got in. "Thank you." She gave him a tired smile. Jessie felt so drained as she worried about her mother. All she could do was hope she'll get better.

The radio came on, and there was a discussion about some politician who was caught cheating on his wife. Jessie said to Seth, "It's incredible how quickly the media moves on. A few days ago, I couldn't even move around."

The traffic light turned green, and the car moved. "Yup. They are always on the next hot topic. I've pretty much gotten used to them."

Jessie nodded and leaned back on the chair. A question popped into her head, and she decided to ask him. "You have the money to get a driver, a home chef, a butler, anything you want, but you don't have any. Why?"

Seth chuckled as he turned into another street. "I'll rather be alone. I've always been a loner since I can remember. I don't like a lot of people being in my space."

Jessie nodded slowly. Now that she had started, she had more questions to ask him. "Also, I've only seen you go to work twice. Why don't you go often?"

Seth grinned as the car turned into Cleveland Avenue. "I own the company. I don't have to go to work when I have employees to handle that. But I have to go more often next week. I'm looking into real estate."

"Is that the deal you want to finalize with Mr. Ferguson?"

Seth nodded as he stopped the car in front of the gate. He brought out his phone and typed in something, then the gate opened, and he drove in. "Yeah. He will be selling to me the lands that I need."

The lights in the garage went off as Seth turned off the ignition of the car. He opened the passenger door for her, and Jessie thankfully smiled at him.

Together, they walked into the house. Jessie felt her head spin and slumped onto the couch. Seth quickly ran to grab her. "Woah! What's wrong?" He set her on the couch, and slowly, Jessie's vision came back. Seth looked at her worriedly. "You're so pale. I think you lost too much blood when Gavin attacked you. You need to rest."

He bent and slowly removed her shoes. "Stay here. I'll get you something to eat." Jessie looked at him with tears in her eyes. He frowned. "Hey, what's wrong?"

She shook her head. "Nothing. It's just that I can't believe this is happening. I've had to deal with everything myself, and this... this feels so great."

Seth kissed her forehead. "I told you. This is how it should be. Now wait here; I'm going to get you something to eat." He walked into the kitchen, and Jessie laid there with her hand on her head.

Not long after, Seth walked in with a plate of steaming chicken soup. The smell of the food made Jessie's stomach growl. All the worrying had made her forget she hadn't eaten much all day.

"Ahhh, here comes the airplane." Jessie giggled as Seth moved the spoonful of chicken soup towards her mouth. She swallowed it and smiled at him with watery eyes. "I love you."

Seth cocked his head and kissed her softly on the lips. "I love you too, Jessie. Now, eat up." Jessie didn't waste any time finishing the bowl of chicken soup.

"Come on, let's get you settled." Seth held her hand and carried her luggage in his other hand as they climbed up the staircase. Jessie paused in front of the guestroom and opened the door to enter.

Seth stopped her. "Where are you going?"

She stared at him, confused. "I can't stay here?"

Seth shook his head. "No, you can't." Then he gave a boyish grin. "You are sleeping in my room; come on."

Jessie blushed and walked into his bedroom. He set her stuff down and grabbed her hand. "Come on. You should take a shower." He led her to his bathroom. Jessie opened the glass door leading to the shower and looked in. She decided to go with the bathtub because she barely had any energy to stand.

Seth turned to leave. "Okay, if you need anything, just let me know. You can regulate the water to your preference with those buttons on the wall."

Jessie held his hand and tilted her head to the bathtub. "Come in with me."

Seth's eyes glazed over as he removed his shirt. Jessie slowly stripped and turned on the water. There was a lavender-scented bathing bomb, and she threw it in. she looked at Seth's naked body as she got into the bubbly water. Seth sat opposite her and looked at her. "This feels nice."

Jessie closed her eyes and nodded. The rhythmic spurts of the water coming out of the Jacuzzi jets massaged her aching body. Jessie was dozing off to sleep when she felt water splash on her face.

She spurted and rapidly opened her eyes.

Seth was grinning and held the lather in his hands.

Jessie blinked at him. "Why?"

He shrugged his muscly shoulders. "Why not?" Jessie scooped some of the lather and threw it at him. He yelped, and a giggle escaped her lips. "Gotcha."

"It's on." Jessie's eyes widened when she saw the size of the lather he threw at her. She closed her eyes as she felt it hit her.

The next few minutes were chaotic. There was water on the floor, and Jessie kept squealing as Seth threw soap at and she did the same.

Seth notices Jessie shiver and grabbed towels. "Come on, let's get out of here." He wrapped Jessie in a towel and wrapped one around himself.

She took out her Peppa pig pajamas, and Seth burst out laughing. "What are you? Twelve?"

Jessie touched her chest in mock insult. "Hey! Those are my favorite." She wore it while sticking out her tongue at him. She still felt weak, but at least she wasn't dizzy anymore.

Seth snickered and wore his silk pajamas before getting into bed. He spread his hands wide. "Come here." Jessie climbed into his embrace and leaned into his warmth.

He started singing an unknown but calming song. Jessie turned to look at him. "What song is that?"

'My mother used to sing it to us when we were little. It used to put us to sleep."

Jessie closed her eyes. "Go on."

His voice was a little shaky, but it was clear. *"Little one, the sun is gone, and the moon is out. Your little bones are tired and need rest."*

Jessie closed her eyes and rested in his arms as he continued to sing.

"So close your eyes and dream of the meadows and hills. Sleep little one, rest your tired bones..." Seth kissed her neck and Jessie bit back a moan. There was something about the way he touched her... made her feel like she could do anything.

She slowly moved her hips on his erection and felt a little bit of satisfaction when she heard him breathe sharply. He held onto her hips and Jessie felt like she was in control. All of a sudden, he picked her up and spun her around. Jessie gasped at the look of want in his eyes. In some minutes, Seth slowly slid into the warm wetness of her and Jessie couldn't hold back a moan this time.

"Oh Seth." She breathes. "Oh Seth."

The bed creaked as they moved faster and faster. When they finally come, they crumble like the waves upon the shores.

Chapter 15

Jessie had woken up to the smell of coffee in the air. She opened her eyes and yawned, focusing her gaze on the hot cup of coffee by her bed. She smiled and took a sip out of it. Seth. Who knew he could be this sweet, despite her first impression of him?

Seth walked into the room wearing a collared long-sleeve shirt tucked into black pants. He had gold cufflinks inserted into his sleeves, and it matched the tiny gold logo on his black brogues. He leaned over and kissed Jessie on the cheek. "Hey you, I'm going to work. You can get anything you want and don't leave the bed too much."

Jessie shook her head and got out of bed. "I don't want to stay in."

Seth cocked an eyebrow. "You almost fainted yesterday; you should be resting."

Jessie shook her head again. "Nah, I feel fine. I want to follow you to work today."

Seth glanced at his Rolex. "Well, okay, if you can get ready in 30 minutes."

Jessie winked at him and ran to the bathroom. She had a quick shower and stared at her hair. She couldn't wash it because it wasn't going to dry on time. She looked into the bathroom cabinet and picked out a leave-in conditioner. She swished mouthwash in her mouth and spat it out.

As she quickly toweled herself out of the shower, she rushed to her luggage and peeped in. "Damn, I need to get more clothes." She muttered to herself. Finally, she pulled out a formal blue dress. She had won it to an event a few years ago and hoped it fit.

"Hey." She called out to Seth, who was doing something on his phone. "Come help me zip this up, please." Seth walked over and tried to zip it up. It only entered when she sucked her belly in.

Seth hid his laughter behind a cough. "You need to get dressed. We'll go shopping after work."

"Okay, I'll buy them."

"But-"

Jessie shook her head. "But nothing. I want to pay for this myself. You have to let me."

Seth hesitated, then nodded. "Fair enough, come on. We need to leave." Jessie grabbed a small purse and applied lip balm before walking out of the house.

Seth walked into the garage and picked out a shiny black Mercedes Benz. Jessie looked at it with admiration, and when Seth caught her staring, he grinned. "She's beautiful, isn't she?" He pressed a button on the key, and the door slid open themselves.

They got into the car and revved out of the compound. Seth was unusually energetic and even bopped to the music playing on the radio.

"What are you so happy about?" Jessie smirked at him.

He laughed. "Nothing much, Just glad you are here." Jessie smiled at him and held his free hand as he drove. Jessie didn't want to ruin his happy mood, but she had to ask. "Seth?"

He turned to look at her. "Yeah?"

"What happened to Gavin's body?" She watched his smile slowly fade away and turned back to the road.

He cleared his throat and spoke. "Well, they buried him already, and that's it."

"How do they work? I mean your meetings or gatherings?"

"Oh, that. We don't have a set timing. We meet at regular intervals when needed. Also, they live in closer range to each other and see quite often, with or without me."

Jessie nodded and decided to end the conversation as soon as the car pulled in front of a tall building. The building was a combination of glass and concrete and towered over the numerous people that walked in and out of the front doors.

Seth got down from the car and held Jessie's hand. "Come on, let's go."

People stopped to greet him. "Good morning, Mr. Irving."

Seth grinned at them. "Jane! Luka! Annie, right? Good morning too." Jessie saw the baffled looks on their faces and suspected that Seth hadn't been so receptive to them before.

The securities at the entrance also looked surprised when Seth greeted them. Jessie took that to notice.

When Jessie got inside the building, she realized just how many people were working for Seth. People raced up and down with phones to their ears or files in their hands. The lobby was expansive, so there was enough space for them to move around. Jessie glanced up and saw the rolls of offices that were behind a glass wall.

Everyone stopped to stare at Jessie as she walked into the room. She smoothened her hair, feeling unconscious with the number of eyes on her. One by one, they all stopped to greet Seth, and he smiled and greeted them back.

"Oh wow, isn't she the woman from the magazine?" Jessie resisted the urge to turn to see the people talking behind her. They walked into the elevator, and Seth pushed the button for the last floor.

"Whew." Jessie played with her dress. "That was something for sure. Your employees seem a little... shell-shocked today." She gave him a pointed look.

Seth ran his hand through his hair. "Ah, that. I admit I haven't been too friendly. I'm working on that."

Jessie agreed. "Yes, you are."

The elevator stopped, and the door opened, revealing the top floor. "And here is my floor. Come on." Jessie walked into space and admired the interior works there. The floor was made up of marble tiles that shone brightly. The cleaners there were doing a great job. The walls were painted a glossy blue, and Jessie felt her heart race faster as she looked through the glass wall down to the lobby.

Seth knocked on an office and pushed the door open. Amelia looked up and smiled brightly when she saw who it was.

She rushed over to them and pulled Jessie into a tight hug. "Oooh, look at you. Welcome to our office. Mr. Irving, welcome back."

Seth smiled at her. "Thank you for assisting me so far. Would have been so disorganized without your help."

Amelia blinked rapidly at Seth's gratitude. "Wow, um, you are always welcome, sir. I have dropped some files on your table. By the way, they need to be signed."

Seth walked out of the room. "Alright, thank you." Jessie turned to look at Amelia and saw her wink at her. She smiled and walked out of the office.

Seth opened the door to his office, and Jessie's eyes widened. It was large. His desk was made of the shiny hook, and the view behind him took Jessie's breath away. It showed a bird-eye view of the city with the building towering over them. A Mini Bar was placed in the corner, and Jessie saw the different wine brands that Seth's company had produced over time.

Right in the corner were a sofa and a small television. Jessie did a little spin. "I could live here."

Seth chuckled and settled right behind his desk. "We won't spend too long here anyway. I just have some files to fill, meetings to attend to, and we're good."

Jessie sat on the sofa opposite him and watched Seth in his element. He had a severe look on his face as he went through the details of his files.

"How did you build your company?" Jessie asked him.

"You know, I'm offended you never googled me. there are countless articles on me."

Jessie smirked at him. "Egotistical much? I never pay much attention to things like that, plus I never had the time."

"Well, I set it up when I was 23. I had to learn everything I did in Asia and launched my own liquor business. I went from bar to bar for the first two years, selling my bottles at crazily low prices. With time and investment, I built it from that point to this moment."

Jessie clapped and wiped away a fake tear. "That was so inspiring, Mr. Irving."

Seth rolled his eyes, but a smile played on his lips. "Of course it is. Everyone, including myself, love that story."

"Huh huh." Jessie snickered and walked up to the mini fridge. She was thirsty, so she just took out a bottle of water. She lifted it to Seth. "Is it okay if I drink this?"

"Of course it is."

Jessie nodded and sat in front of the TV. She scrolled through the channel before settling on a soap opera.

Seth spoke to her. "Hey, I'm going for a meeting; I'll be back."

"Okay, bye." She waved at him as he left the room. Thirty minutes later, Jessie was wholly invested in the film.

Seth walked back into the room and said to her, "Come on, let's go."

Jessie held up a finger to him while still concentrating on the movie. "No, No. Angelo is about to reveal himself to Julia. I have to finish this."

Seth sighed and plopped into the seat beside her. "What it's about?"

"Okay so, Lucia was in love with a man called Gabriel, and they had the sweetest relationship. One night, she had a car accident, and her memory was wiped away. Then she met Angelo and fell in love with him. But what she doesn't know is that Gabriel is also Angelo!"

A few minutes after, Seth was also invested in the film. Finally, the credits rolled by, and Seth stood up and applauded. "That was good. I don't remember the last time I watched anything on Tv."

Jessie did a little courtesy. "Well, you are welcome."

"Now, can we go?" Jessie nodded at his question, and together, they walked out of the room. As they passed Amelia's office, Jessie opened the door and smiled at her. "Hey, we're heading out. I'll see you soon, bye."

Amelia waved at her and Seth. "Okay, bye."

They rode the elevator and arrived at the lobby. Although not many people stared at them, they still attracted a couple of curious stares. Thankfully, they walked out of the building and up to the car. Jessie got into her seat, and Seth turned the ignition and drove out of the parking lot.

"There's this place downtown that I think you'll like. It's called Madeline's." Seth said to Jessie, and she opened her mouth to say her usual purchases are from the local thrift store, but her cheeks burnt red when she thought about it. It was a better option to buy more quality clothes.

The store wasn't far from the office because they stopped in front of a small but beautiful shop a few turns later. Mannequins inside a glass rocked different outfits that Jessie couldn't help but admire. They got down from the car, and a cheerful lady walked up to them. Her eyes widened a bit when she recognized them, but Jessie admired that she kept her composure.

"Hi, welcome to Madeline's! my name is Camilla. We have dresses, blouses, skirts, pants; you name it. What are you interested in?"

Jessie replied. "Oh, I'm looking to buy clothes in general. I want to change my wardrobe."

Camilla nodded. "Of course, right this way." She led to a separate section, and Jessie looked at the dresses hanging from their various lines. She smiled and nodded when she saw them, and they were just what she wanted.

"You like them?" Seth asked her. Jessie nodded in response and picked out a flowery dress that stopped at her thighs. She also picked out some formal dresses in case they were needed. But most of the clothes she chose were cute dresses; she couldn't get enough of those. She took them all into the dressing room and tried them one by one. She only returned one blouse to the line because she didn't like how it looked on her.

She walked up to Camilla and handed her the clothes she had bought. Camilla smiled at her pile. "Awesome choices, ma'am."

"t\Thank you." While Camilla was calculating the cost, Jessie walked up to the jewelry stand. She had her eyes set on a particular necklace. It was made of gold, and the tiny pendant was an opal held up by two hands. She liked it and checked the tag attached to it. Jessie dropped the necklace like it was hot coal.

Two hundred dollars for a tiny necklace? She gritted her teeth and walked back to where Camilla was bagging her clothes. "That will be $542."

Jessie wanted to take it all back, but she decided to do this one thing for herself, so she handed over her credit card. Seth walked away. "I'll be back, and I need to use the restroom. Just wait for me by the car."

With that, he walked away.

Camilla grinned at Jessie. "Ma'am, you are so lucky. I can't believe the tabloids said you were faking. You both are adorable." Jessie couldn't help but blush and smile back.

"Thank you very much."

"Of course. Here's your bag. Please thank you for shopping with Madeline's, and have an amazing day."

Jessie thanked her and walked out of the building. The car was locked, so she rested against it, with the bag placed on the hood. Then, she heard the sound of a camera clicking. Jessie turned her head just in time to see a man holding a camera to her face. When he realized she had seen him, he bounced off.

"Hey!" Jessie called out, but he was already gone.

A few minutes after, Seth walked out of the building. "I heard you yell. Are you okay?"

Jessie nodded. "Just some crazy photographer."

"Ah, them. They were bound to find out anyway. Come on, let's get out of here."

They entered the car and drove away. Jessie's phone rang, and when she opened it to look at it, it was Lucy. She bit her lip with guilt but picked the call. "Hey, Lucy. I am so sorry."

Lucy laughed breezily. "It's okay, honestly. How are you doing?"

Jessie rubbed her forehead. "Honestly, not so good. My mom relapsed, and she's still unconscious at the hospital."

"Oh god! I am so sorry. I do hope she gets better."

"Me too."

Jessie hesitated before saying the next thing she wanted to say. "Um, I don't know if this is a good time, but I wanted to remind you that Aaron's career day is coming, and... I don't know if you still have someone." She added in a rush. "It's okay if you don't; I can tell him not to worry about it."

Jessie hit her forehead silently. "No! It's still on. Don't worry."

"Oh, thanks so much!"

"It's nothing really. Take care and greet the kids and Bobo, okay?"

Lucy said her goodbyes and hung up. Seth looked at her curiously. "Who was that?"

"My friend, Lucy. Um, Seth, would you be able to attend a child's career day." She shook her head. "It's okay if you don't want to. You're busy and all-"

"It's okay." He smiled as he drove the car. "I'll be there. Just tell me the date and time. I'll add it to my schedule."

"Oh, thank you. It's next week Tuesday, and I'm not sure about the time, I'll ask. Thank you again!"

Seth opened his mouth to talk, but his phone rang. Connected to the Bluetooth, he picked up, and Amelia's voice filled the room. "Hey, Amelia, what's up?"

"Um, sir, we have an emergency meeting. James Addison from the California branch is here right now, and it seems essential. I haven't heard much from him, but it seems like there's a problem with the branch.

Seth frowned and slowed the car. "Like right now?"

"Yes, sir."

"Okay, I'm on my way." The call ended, and he turned to Jessie. "let's go back to the office."

Jessie shook her head. She wasn't sure she would have much to do when he was in the office. "Nah, I think I want to hang out here for some time." There were rolls of stores that lined the streets, and she hadn't even been aware of them. She wanted to explore a bit.

Seth frowned. "Are you sure about that? You're still recovering, you know?"

"I feel much better. Plus, I'll just go home when I'm tired." Home. Jessie liked the way that rolled off the top of her mouth.

Seth hesitated but nodded. "Call if anything happens, anything at all." He kissed her on the left cheek before driving away. Jessie waved at the car as it zoomed off.

She walked down the streets and looked into the shops. There was a pastry shop, and the smell of cakes made her enter it. Jessie opened the door and walked into the store. Lines of cake models were arranged in front of the windows, and cupcakes were inside the transparent glass. A sweet-looking old woman smiled at Jessie as she walked in. "Hello, how may I help you?"

"I'll like a slice of fudge cake and some orange juice."

The woman nodded, and Jessie waited till she put the cake on a plate. She didn't feel comfortable letting the elderly woman serve her while she just waited at the table.

"Aww, thank you for being patient. This is on the house."

Jessie smiled at her. "Oh wow, thank you for that." She sneakily dropped the exact amount of the food in the tip box and walked out of the shop. She bit into the cake and moaned; it was so good. Jessie ate it and sipped the orange juice when her eyes sighted something.

It was a dog shelter just tucked right in the corner of the roll of shops. "How come I haven't seen this before?" She muttered to herself. She walked up to the building and pushed the door open. A surly teenager stared at her and turned back to his magazine. Well, that was rude, Jessie thought to herself. He didn't bother asking her what she wanted.

It was a small room, but rows and rows of dogs all lined up around him. Some were asleep, some looked uninterested, some were restless, and some looked happy. The mood in the room was so gloomy that it dampened Jessie's mood.

Finally, the teenager was tired of ignoring her. He talked to her in a tone that suggested he had said it so many times. "My name is Drew; what dog will you like to see?"

"As many as I can."

He cocked a brow at her reply but shrugged. He walked up to the front door and shut it. Seeing Jessie's expression, he explained why. "We don't have enough space in here, and we can't afford to set the dogs loose.

Jessie nodded and pointed to an uninterested terrier. She sat on the floor and blinked at Jessie. Drew knelt and unlocked her cage. He squinted at her, the name tag on her neck. "This one is Barbie."

Jessie slowly walked up to the dog and knelt before her. She talked to Barbie in a calm tone. "Hey girl, a pretty name you got."

The terrier cocked her head at the sound of Jessie's voice. She moved closer and sniffed Jessie's dress. She scratched behind Barbie's ears, and she slowly wagged her tail. Jessie grinned at her. "You like that, don't you?" Soon, Drew returned the terrier to her cage.

The dogs that followed weren't as bad as they seemed. They were only bored and tired of being in such an enclosed space. She tried to keep their names in her head. Drake, Luna, Alla, Cooper, and Max. Drew shook his head when she pointed at Max's cage. "Him? Nah. He's not going to come out. He has been that way since he got here."

Jessie ignored him and sat by his cage. Max laid on the floor with his eyes turned to the wall. He completely ignored her.

His cage was big enough for her to enter, so she crawled in and sat in it, keeping some distance between them so he wouldn't get scared.

Max was a white and black boxer doodle and had a little white spot on his forehead that roughly looked like a star. Jessie sat there and talked to him. She recounted all her experiences with dogs as a child and how she had once witnessed a dog give birth; it was the most memorable event she held highly.

Max didn't look interested, but Jessie knew he was listening. She glanced outside and saw that Drew was staring at her curiously. Slowly, Max stood up and moved closer to Jessie. He laid his head on her lap and closed his eyes.

Drew's jaws dropped. "No way."

Jessie softly stroke Max. "He is very stressed and has probably been on his own for too long. He just needs company." She sat there, inside the cage, and talked to the dog. He stared at her with his soulful eyes as she spoke to him.

Her phone rang and interrupted a story about how she had snuck out an abused dog from its owner's home. She looked at the number on the screen. It was Mandy. "Hello?" Jessie picked up the call.

"Jessie. Your mother is awake!"

Chapter 16

It had been a week since Hannah woke up, and Jessie had spent all her time beside her. Although she couldn't leave yet, Doctor Lucas said she wouldn't spend so long in the hospital. "With adequate treatment, she will live a long life," were his exact words.

Seth had also come around as often as possible, and Hannah wouldn't stop teasing Jessie about him. "Well, well, well, I thought it was just the media. Look at you, glowing." Hannah hadn't lost her sharp tongue despite what she had been through.

Jessie rolled her eyes but smiled. "Who says it's not just for the tabloids?"

Hannah cocked a brow at her. "Your entire expression says it's real. You are obviously in love with that man."

Jessie opened her mouth to argue, but it was true. She was in love with Seth. The way his eyes lit up when he saw something he liked, the way he took the other shifters like brothers, even though they almost killed him, the way he would place his head on her laps after shapeshifting and going for a run, the way he never seemed to let her go. She loved all of it.

But one thing she loved the most about him was how he motivated her to pursue her dreams. He was relentlessly working on building his estates across the country, and Jessie couldn't help but admire his motivation, which was why she decided to apply as a caregiver at the dog shelter.

The owner was a retired bet doctor, and he seemed happy to have someone take all the workload from him. Also, Drew needed help, and even though he was still as sullen as ever, he had been warming up to her slowly.

Jessie adjusted the brooch on her mother's cashmere sweater. Hannah was glad she didn't have to wear the hospital dress. "Dratted thing", she always called it. Hannah looked down at the brooch shaped like a flower and smiled. "Thanks for this again."

"It was your birthday, mom, and you are always welcome." She placed her head on Hannah's forehead. "I'm so glad you are here. I'm not sure what I would do if it hadn't been for you."

Hannah kissed her on the cheek. "I would never leave you, not yet. I love you too, my baby."

A knock interrupted their conversation, and Seth walked in, holding some fresh pansies in his hands. He wore sneakers, and Jessie raised her brow at the unusual combo of Jeans and a T-shirt.

He shrugged. "What? I wanted to look cool."

Jessie snickered. "Huh huh, how was it?" He had fulfilled his promise and went for Aaron's career day. Lucy had called her earlier and thanked her profusely. Jessie missed her and scheduled a picnic later in the weekend. It was high time she introduced Seth to one of her favorite people.

"It was quite interesting. The kids are genius and bombarded me with questions. Let's say Aaron is now the most popular kid at school." Seth brushed off imaginary dust from his shoulders.

"Show off," Jessie said to him, but she did a little flip inside her. She was certain she had finally won Aaron to her side.

Hannah watched their exchange with a smile, and Seth walked up to her. He kissed her on her cheek. "How do you feel?"

"Oh, you know, the usual." Hannah rolled her eyes, but Jessie knew that her mother approved of Seth very much. Seth also liked her a lot and wouldn't stop buying her gifts, despite the fact the both Hannah and Jessie had protested against it.

"Well, we need to go. I'll see you soon, mom." Jesse gave her mother a tight hug and proceeded to leave the room. She wasn't sure what happened next, but what Jessie knew was that she felt her head spin in the next second, and everything went black.

"She's awake; she's awake." Jessie woke up to the sound of different people in the room. Nina beamed at her, and Mandy was holding her hands to her heart.

She turned to look at the person who mattered the most, Seth. He had unshed tears in his eyes, and Jessie's heart raced faster. Did something happen to her? What she ill?

A woman, who was the doctor, walked into the room. "Okay, people, give her some space." She gave Jessie a reassuring smile and felt a hand to her head. "You have nothing to worry about." She handed Jessie a slip of paper. Jessie tried to read it, but none of it made sense.

"I'm sorry, what's this about?"

Seth couldn't hold it in, so he blurted out. "Baby, you're pregnant. You are pregnant with my child."

Jessie blinked rapidly, unsure of what she had just heard. She looked at the doctor for confirmation, and the doctor nodded. "Yes, Ms. Lewis, you are two weeks pregnant."

A teardrop fell from Jessie's eyes, and she shed tears of joy. She gently placed a hand on her stomach. She was going to be a mom. Jessie threw her hands around Seth. "I can't believe it. Oh my god."

Seth cleaned her tears and looked into her eyes. "I love you so much."

"I love you too." Jessie had never been too particular about many things, but for once, she felt complete.

THE END